DO YOU WANT TO BE SEDUCED?

Darcy boisterously jolted Claire's horse with his as they rode down the forest path. Breathlessly, he said, "You ride like a centaur. We should make love like centaurs."

Claire was fairly sure that Desmarais was joking. She had no fear of him, as she had written him down as a trifler. Still she was thrilled by her exercise.

"With centaurs—is it not just the horse part that makes love?" she retorted.

Darcy laughed. "Then the human part must be innocent," he said, reaching for her to kiss her. Startled, Claire brought her whip down across his horse's nose. Then she looked up and saw Lord Ross approaching through the trees.

"I . . ." she began.

"Never mind, I saw what happened," he said angrily. "You have been behaving like a shameless tease. Do you want to be seduced?"

RAKE'S REWARD

Madeline Gibson

BANTAM BOOKS
TORONTO · NEW YORK · LONDON

RAKE'S REWARD
A Bantam Book / July 1981

ISBN 0-553-13191-5

Published simultaneously in the United States
and Canada

Bantam Books are published by Bantam Books, Inc.
Its trademark, consisting of the words "Bantam Books"
and the portrayal of a bantam, is Registered in U.S.
Patent and Trademark Office and in other countries.
Marca Registrada. Bantam Books, Inc., 666 Fifth
Avenue, New York, New York 10103.

PRINTED IN THE UNITED STATES OF AMERICA

0 9 8 7 6 5 4 3 2 1

Chapter 1

The candles in the sconces along the wall were burning low, and some of them had guttered, throwing the elegant supper room of the African into unaccustomed gloom. Viscount Darcy Desmarais reached for the brandy bottle, trailing his fine lace cuff through a plate of peas. His companion Colin Quartermayne drew the bottle farther away. "You're foxed enough," he told his friend. On the other side of the table, Lord Edward Ashton smiled wearily. He did not much like the newly arrived Quartermayne, even though he was heir to an Irish peerage, but that cub Darcy did need someone to tell him when to stop.

With a sudden movement Desmarais flipped the bottle out of Quartermayne's hands into the air. It turned end over end, spilling a few drops, and landed right side up in Desmarais's lap. His friend laughed.

"Blister me if I know how you do it," said Lord Ashton.

"Practice, m'boy," mumbled Desmarais, refilling his glass.

Ashton frowned indulgently. "You'll practice yourself into an early grave. Have you seen George Howard?"

"He's winning at *vingt-et-un*, at the high table—the bastard," grumbled Desmarais.

"Is Howard the man in gray, the tall cool one?" asked Quartermayne.

"Yes," said Lord Ashton, looking askance at the Irishman in his mulberry satin coat. "But if you knew him, you would not call him cool."

"Howard was winning all right, and *he* was losing." Quartermayne gestured toward his young host with just the trace of a sneer.

1

"Speaking of gray," said Desmarais impudently, "did you know he only has four suits?"

"You're always watching him," said Ashton. "Why waste your time?"

Desmarais's already handsome face became even more appealing as an abandoned smile spread over it. "I admire winners," he retorted. Then a wicked and satirical glint came into his eyes, and he began to sing. . . .

> —and George of Ross
> is never at a loss
> till he takes a toss
> at Charing Cross!

He gestured expansively with his glass and as his eye followed his hand, it fell on the immaculate figure of a man in pale gray evening clothes with a vest embroidered in white cornflowers. Desmarais's tapered fingers went limp and the glass fell. A servant rushed forward to tidy up the mess, while the gentleman advanced to the table. Desmarais's eyes had not followed his glass of brandy, on its fatal plunge. They remained fixed in the ironical, sapphire-hard stare of the newcomer. Quartermayne stiffened. He was not sure why, but knew an insult had just been extended. He feared that this George whatever it was might call his friend out, and although robust and adroit, he had no taste for duels, even as a second.

However, the newcomer simply began to fill a plate with food, and Desmarais drawled, "Quartermayne, may I make you known to the luckiest frequenter of all the hells from highest to lowest: George Howard? Howard, may I present Colin Quartermayne, Viscount Allenvale?"

"It is *your* presence which brings me luck," said Mr. Howard, and Desmarais winced. Then Howard turned to Quartermayne. "Delighted to make your acquaintance, sir."

Quartermayne smiled ingratiatingly. "Are you by any chance brother to Edward Howard, Baron Ross?" he asked.

Howard bowed slightly over his plate. "That is my

2

misfortune," he said gravely, "but I warn you that I share neither my brother's wealth nor his patronage." Desmarais grinned. It was not often that Quartermayne was set down for being inquisitive.

Ashton frowned again as he watched the brother of the foreign office favorite calmly attacking his meal. Howard was not usually so blunt. But Lord Ross had cut his younger brother off five years before, and nothing irritated George more than to be compared with him.

"Stap me, if I ate as much as you do, Howard, I'd get terribly fat," Ashton said, in a clumsy attempt to change the subject.

"You're terribly fat already, Ashton," replied Howard.

Desmarais put in, "Did you know Sylvia was in town? *She* has got really fat!"

"Which Sylvia?" asked Howard innocently.

"How many could there have been?" sneered Desmarais. Quartermayne reached into the pocket of his coat for his snuff box.

Howard picked up a napkin and stared pensively at the chandelier. "Sylvia Bowie, at school. Remember, Ashton, in your room? . . . Sylvia Knight, Sylvia Demarest, Lady Sylvia Davenham, Countess Sylvie D'Arblay—but no, you said Sylvia, not Sylvie. . . ." Lord Ashton laughed, and Quartermayne sneezed violently. He wondered if Howard were indeed boasting the conquests of so many ladies.

"Sylvia Cameron," said Desmarais intensely. "I'd have thought you'd remember. She had her son with her."

"Was that the Scottish lady we met?" asked Quartermayne. "Pretty, but her child is a pestilential brat."

"All children are pestilential brats, and mine in particular," said Ashton, trying to change the subject again, noticing how tightly the napkin was clenched in Howard's hand. Surely if Desmarais had been that impertinent to him, Lord Ashton would have shut him up long before this.

At that moment, a man, obviously not a gentleman, crossed the room and shyly approached the supper table. With a deep bow he handed a letter to

3

Howard, who glared at him and ordered him to get his carcase out into the hall. Howard read the message and crumpled it in his hand Then he stood up. "I beg your pardon, gentlemen, but I think I must now take my leave," he said with a wry smile. "I shall see you about the horses tomorrow, Ashton, if I may."

"Good night, Howard," said Lord Ashton, and his friend bowed and walked slowly to the door, leaving the crumpled paper on the tablecloth.

"An urgent summons from Lady Montgomery!" said Desmarais recklessly, but Howard was already out of earshot.

"No, no. From Lady Hartfield," said Ashton, laughing.

"But we really must bet," proposed Desmarais. "I'll wager a monkey it is from la Montgomery."

"Done," said Lord Ashton, but both men hesitated to unfold the piece of paper. Up in the world as they were, it still did not seem quite the gentlemanly thing to do.

At last Quartermayne reached for it, smoothed it out, and read them the news that Edward Howard, Baron Ross, had died in Switzerland of an assassin's bullet through his lung. George Howard was the new Baron Ross. Ashton took a close look at the seal; it was genuine.

"And you say he isn't cool," said Quartermayne in awe. "He walked out of here as if it were of no importance at all!"

The heavy rain was still falling when Edward Ashton left the African and, hailing the only available cab, went home to bed. He was the only one of the three to have known the dead man and the only one to grieve—not because he would miss Baron Ross's company, but because the Regency had lost an irreplaceable man. Ashton felt uneasy because he had won money over it.

"Damn Ashton, anyway," said Colin Quartermayne peevishly, buttoning his cloak. "Couldn't he have shared?"

"He goes the other way," said Desmarais. "Besides,

4

it's only the smallest distance." Desmarais began slogging home through the puddles with wild élan, showing no care for the finish on his boots or for the mud he splashed on his companion. Quartermayne drew his cloak closer around him.

"Desmarais, what was Sylvia Cameron to Howard anyhow?"

"I'm a pig, Quartermayne. I will tease him. The devil knows why I do it."

"I know. You admire winners," said Quartermayne ironically.

Desmarais took his friend by the shoulders. "I don't tell this to everybody, but he's a gambler. That's how he lives! If he cheats, I've never heard of it—and it was my fault his brother disowned him."

Quartermayne shifted uncomfortably in his damp cloak. The revelation that Mr. George Howard had paid the price of his dissolute behavior by being disowned was not sufficiently interesting to compensate for the devastation the rain was wreaking on his "windswept" hairstyle. He wondered bleakly if his acquaintance with this abandoned puppy was worth it.

Desmarais released his victim and walked on. They were now only a few streets from his sister's house.

"How could it be your fault?" inquired Quartermayne, stretching himself to match Desmarais's pace.

"I collided with him in my rig," called out Desmarais, "wrecked his phaeton. Threw him and Miss Cameron down, and a great crowd of people came up. Impossible to hide the fact that she'd been meeting him secretly. Cameron had her married off to Lord Ogilvie within a fortnight. Poor Howard. He planted me a facer over that, and I called him out, but he missed me. Now I say whatever I like to him."

"Wait!" called Quartermayne. Desmarais had broken into a run. "Wait, will you?"

Desmarais turned and stopped, a little out of breath. He nervously stirred the water in a nearby puddle with his cane. "Dreadful scandal about Miss Cameron, the duel, all that. Lot of nasty talk and Ross believed it all. Cut his brother off without a penny and refused to listen to a word of explanation.

5

George Howard sold his hunters and went back to his regiment."

"Best thing for him, I think," said Quartermayne.

"He was wounded at Badajoz and still wasn't fit enough to go back. Papa should have let me go." Desmarais began to run again.

"You'd have got your head shot off!" said Quartermayne.

"I would not. I've a good head. Know how to keep it!"

"You're not going to want to keep it tomorrow morning!" shouted Quartermayne, pressing on in Desmarais's splattered wake, so as not to be outdistanced in unfamiliar streets, where his friend could pass with charmed ease, but where he alone would certainly be set on and robbed.

Chapter 2

George Howard was far from suspecting that his fortunes were being shouted through the damp, uncaring streets. In front of the mirror in his small chilly room Howard undressed with his usual care. He had had to be careful of his things for so long now that it had become habit. Stripped of his embroidered waistcoat and elegant cravat, his body seemed leaner than before. It's a good thing Ashton doesn't know that the supper I get in the hells is often my only meal all day, thought the new Baron Ross, grinning at his dimly lit image in the glass.

"Lord Ross," he bowed to himself and laughed harshly, revealing a row of perfect teeth. Unable to even think of sleep, he paced up and down the room in his stockings. Now he was master of Oakhaven. He doubted if Edward had left him a single pound, so heartily had his brother disapproved of his style of life. Still, he would inherit the title and the estate, with the considerable rents it could bring. Yet when George Howard thought of Oakhaven he did not usually think of rents. He had accustomed himself to think of the good times, when he and his father had ridden over the estate, making stops to watch a covey of partridge chicks or for him to climb a certain tree while his father watched. In winter he had learned to shoot, but better than shooting, George had loved the beauty of the icy sunrises. At Christmas there had been hot punch and mummers. . . .

He glanced at himself again with dissatisfaction. He was now Baron Ross, and what was there to recommend him? He had expended his best efforts and all of his money to be accepted in society as a man of fashion, riding with the Quorn simply because it was stylish, and catering to the whims of Lady Montgomery when he would have preferred a wife of his own.

Although he had passionately hated his brother, George could not rejoice. His brother's death had brought on an attack of grief for his parents, who had been carried off by typhus when he was eight, leaving him at Edward's mercy. Now that Edward had died, there was no one left living who would call George by his Christian name. Baron Ross! The title he had grown to hate was now his own.

Pacing about the room, George thought again of Lady Patricia Leland, the unattainable lady he and a dozen other gentlemen had pursued all last season. George flattered himself that of all her beaux he had been most favored, but that meant nothing in the face of Lord Leland's impossibly high standards. Whoever married his daughter had to be young, handsome, rich, titled, *and* of impeccable reputation. It seemed that in Lord Cedric Leland's view, his daughter—chaste, religious, delicate, and witty—was too good for the best of them. Perhaps Lady Patricia had returned from Scotland, although the season had not yet begun. If it had not been for that cursed Cameron scandal . . .

George did not decide lightly to offer for the fair Patricia. He had never proposed marriage before, nor had he gone without companionship because of this. There had been many willing girls and married women from whom he had parted on good terms. Their secrets had always been scrupulously kept—except once, when that fool Darcy Desmarais ran into his phaeton. Desmarais still believes I was in love with her, he thought. Let him; but I envy her her children. She's probably an excellent mother. George searched his face in the glass, looking for a resemblance to his mother, Cecelia, and longed for a child who could love him as he had loved her. Staring back from the dark mirror, he saw a hard intense face made sinister by the saber cut he had received in Spain. Nevertheless Lady Patricia had said that she liked his face.

Impulsively, the new Lord Ross polished his own boots and put on his black coat, the one he wore when disguised as a merchant in order to speculate

8

on 'change. It was five o'clock when he donned his better cloak and began walking toward Westminister. In the abbey he said a prayer for his mother and another out of thankfulness for the end of his scrounging life. There was no honor in being in the army in time of peace, but since selling his commission, George had been hard put to it to conceal the depths of his indigence. Everyone knew he had no great estate, and many would think that his offer for Lady Patricia was prompted by her fortune.

George sat for a long time until the sun's rays began to shine through the rose windows, and the acolytes began to prepare the altar for the early service. What difference if the ton thought him a fortune hunter, so long as the Lelands knew otherwise? Sweet Patricia. She was no child and had no false missish airs. Indeed it was her third season, and if it had not been for Lord Cedric's intransigence, she would certainly have been married long ago. Patricia was so graceful in all her movements, so delicate of feature, so honest in her desire for him. Yet she had always been discreet. It had required all his control not to compromise her.

At the end of the service an old gentleman from the foreign office saw George Howard leave the abbey, looking extremely abstracted. Poor lad, he thought. It's hit him hard. Ross was such a fine man.

Chapter 3

At that moment the object of George Howard's intentions stood opposite a window overlooking St. James's Park. Instead of gazing out into the hazy morning sun, Lady Patricia Leland held herself motionless, while Anne laced her into the new stays modish ladies were just starting to wear. She hid the thrill she felt at the change they made in her shape—the emphasis they gave her perfectly rounded breasts and already tiny waist. It was not until Anne had finished with her buttons and was dismissed that Lady Patricia permitted herself an admiring glance in the glass.

Lord Leland did not approve of her favorite styles, and the dress she was wearing was modesty itself. He's such an anchorite, she thought, but when I am married no one will tell me what I may wear. In fact marriage now seemed more attractive than it had in her first season or her second. She was glad that her mother had become ill, and their tedious tour of Scotland had been cut short. The Scottish lads were such mannerless wretches, and some of them were outright Francophiles! No. It was better in London, where every day brought some new excitement, intrigue, or opportunity to alter events by placing a word at the right time, in the right ear. Lady Patricia had worked to master this art, and now she itched to exercise her mastery.

Quietly Patricia descended to the landing so as not to attract the attention of her father, who might very well take the opportunity to assign her some literary task to improve her mind.

Nothing and nobody, she thought with contempt, is ever good enough for Lord Leland. He should go to heaven with all the other saints! As she thought this,

Lady Patricia flinched with guilt as if her father, behind his paneled library doors, could read her mind. As she passed the library, she could hear her father's voice, speaking in cadenced tones to some early visitor. If I were Papa, she thought, I wouldn't do dreary business before breakfast. Then she turned and went down to eat.

George knew that Lord Leland rose early and would not be discommoded by an early call, but still he was surprised by the kindness with which he was received. Lord Leland was a bit retiring but he did not merit Patricia's epithet "anchorite." He had an extremely wide acquaintance in the House of Lords and kept well up on doings in society. He deliberately maintained this knowledge to spare his wife and daughter the distress of making unsuitable acquaintances, like that (most recently) of Caroline Lamb. In this endeavor Lord Leland had been so successful that his daughter came close to crediting him with second sight. Because of his vigilance, Lord Ross, like Lady Patricia's other beaux, was not a little in awe of him.

Instead of beginning with inquiries about George's somewhat questionable means or his highly questionable morals, Leland began with, "Why do you want to marry my daughter?" George was caught somewhat off guard.

"I think she's the most fascinating woman I've ever met," was all he could think of to say.

"And?"

"Uh . . . I admire her mind. Lady Patricia really understands people. . . . She's entertaining to be with. . . . I could never bear being married to a stupid woman."

"Indeed. Do you love her?" Lord Leland's cornflower-blue eyes, cool and penetrating, closely resembled his daughter's, and like hers they had an unsettling effect.

"I think I do. You see, your grace, I don't think I've ever been in love before. This is the first offer I . . ."

"I doubt that very much," interjected Lord Leland.

George grinned uncomfortably. "The first honorable

11

offer, I should have said. Don't you think we would have beautiful children?"

Smiling at the earnest confusion on George Howard's handsome face, Lord Leland couldn't help feeling that he had a point. But when he thought of Patricia's coldness to her nieces, his expression hardened. George read refusal in it and was not surprised. Lord Leland had refused wealthy, titled men before.

Leland was frowning when he began to speak. "You may court Patricia on these conditions: You must observe a three-month period of mourning for your brother. You must reduce your gambling and sever all immoral connections you may have. If at the end of three months I find your conduct to have been above reproach, you may make your offer, and we can discuss a financial settlement at that time. Of course you realize that I would never force Patricia to marry against her wishes, nor would I see her poorly connected. Too unequal a situation would not be right for her or for you. It is to your credit that you had the forbearance to wait, because my daughter has £10,000 a year. Circumstanced as you were yesterday, I should have had to refuse you outright." He paused, then said more cordially, "Patricia has mentioned you often, and with liking."

George took his leave of Lord Leland with an odd floating feeling. Although the effects of the brandy he had taken hours before were certainly worn off, he felt light-headed. As his eyes beheld Lady Patricia Leland's ascent of the stair, he became truly intoxicated.

Her charming uptilted nose wrinkled and her lips parted in a delightful smile. She noticed wryly that it was her father he had come to see. She supposed it was a money matter, probably a gambling debt, and sneered inwardly, but she said, "I do not think black is your color, Mr. Howard."

"Not mine, Lady Patricia, my brother's. Lord Ross is dead."

Lady Patricia gave a little shriek of pleasure, and glancing around quickly to see if they were observed, planted a light kiss on George's cheek. "Felicitations,

12

my lord Baron," she whispered. Then she continued to mount the stair. George caught a glimpse of the delicate lace of her petticoat. He went after her two steps at a time and placed himself in her way. He put his large strong hands on each side of her tiny waist.

"Let me go at once, sir," Lady Patricia demanded calmly. "Mama is coming down in a moment and she will see us."

"You shall not elude me that easily. Stand and deliver!" he said imperiously. It was a game of George's to play at highwayman, but only for kisses. She averted her face, but to no avail. His head turned with hers and caught her mouth. She felt her body melting—but this was not a good place or time for dalliance.

"La, Mr. Howard. I shall have to spend another half hour arranging my hair," she complained without rancor.

"Lady Patricia, when your father permits me to offer for you, will you be my wife?" he asked, grinning at her surprise.

"*Lord Ross* . . . my father has not given permission?" There was an undercurrent of excitement in her disbelief.

"A vast indiscretion on his part, I am sure," answered the baron. "One he will doubtless regret. If you agree to it, he will miss you desperately. One cannot help missing you, Patricia."

Her eyes were sparkling as she put her smooth white finger across his mouth. It smelled faintly of roses.

"Hush, my lord. You must not call me Patricia. If we were married I should be Lady Ross, but for now I must still be Lady Patricia."

"If? Pray do not tease me," said George, a little shocked that she would think first of names at such a time. Perhaps she did not care for him after all.

"What did Papa say to you?" she asked seriously.

This was not quite what he expected her to say, but he responded with the gist of her father's conversation. When he finished, he stared hopefully into her beautiful distant blue eyes.

"Yes, my lord," she said evenly. "I would accept

your offer. But three months of mourning will surely be tiresome. And your card partners will be furious! I wouldn't wonder if they came begging for you to fleece them. Do you think you can bear it?" Her lips, with the merest soupçon of a smile, were at once pure and provocative. He longed to crush them under his own, again and again. Patricia felt the tiniest bit afraid. His eyes, under their dark, irregular brows, seemed a little dangerous. Just as George reached for her again there was a sound on the landing. Nimbly, Lady Patricia hopped out of her suitor's reach. At that moment, bewitched by her lightness, delicacy and wit, George lost his balance and sank with his bad knee against the stair.

Looking down, Lady Leland saw George Howard, one of the more obvious fortune hunters of her acquaintance. "On your knees before beauty, sir?" she said severely.

Painfully George rose to his feet.

"Mama," Lady Patricia began.

"I'm surprised, miss. Wasting your time with gentlemen, when you knew I was waiting!" Lady Leland looked over the rail with as much hauteur as her short stature would permit.

"Mama, Lord Ross has succeeded to his brother's title, and Papa is going to allow him to offer for me when his mourning period is over," said her daughter dryly.

"His lordship gave me permission to speak to her," said George.

"And?" Lady Leland tilted a challenging glance at her daughter.

"I plan to accept, Mama," said Lady Patricia, looking askance at George, whose glowing smile told her that her moment of courage was appreciated. He knew how much in awe of her parents Lady Patricia was.

George took two steps upward and seized her hand gently, bending to kiss her slender fingers. "Your father said I might not visit you just at first, because of the mourning. I will go to Oakhaven and put it in order for you. Promise you will visit me!"

"If Papa permits, I would like very much to see the place—but you do not mean we should live in the

14

country?" A note of doubt, almost of horror, crept into her voice.

George laughed. "Not if you do not wish it," he said. "I shall write to you every day."

Patricia frowned and smiled at the same time. "Yes, you must," she said firmly, pulling her pearl-ringed fingers out from under his strong brown ones. She was very much aware of her mother's disapproval.

"*Au revoir*," said George, and began his descent, followed by two pairs of eyes—one which wanted him to go, and the other, to stay.

When George was safely out of earshot, Lady Leland turned to Patricia and said, "Have you lost your senses, Patricia? I think Cedric has taken leave of his!"

Lady Patricia went to get her cloak and hat. She calmly put them on, turned to her mother, and said with resolution, "I favor the match for a number of reasons." Her mother adjusted her hat before the gilt-framed glass in the lower hall, being careful not to disarrange her wig in the process.

"His extreme wealth, for instance," said Lady Leland. ". . . Or perhaps it is his spotless reputation which attracts you?"

Patricia turned to her mother spitefully as they went out. "It is no good being sarcastic, Mama. Why Papa did not refuse him, I cannot guess, but I am glad! George adores me. If we were married, he would not make me obey him. I do not want a husband who would plague my life out—like Papa. Lord Ross is handsome and I love him and with my money, we would be rich enough."

Lady Leland gave her daughter a hard look. It was true that as the richer partner, Patricia could perhaps retain control, but knowing her daughter, she was not sure this was wise.

"We shall buy Lord Morson's house," said Patricia with decision.

"I think it is hideous," said Lady Leland. "Your father would never approve."

"The Morson house is the *dernier cri*," retorted Patricia. "And after we are married, Papa will have nothing to say about what we do."

15

Lady Leland sighed. She had hoped that Patricia might do better than a mere baron. However, it could have been worse. Her eldest girl had been totally disowned and the family forbidden to mention her name. Lady Leland wondered with a pang if Lydia and the subaltern she had married were still alive and well in India. She wondered if Patricia had been thinking of them, too. Perhaps her daughter wasn't being so stupid. Why shouldn't she prefer to rule her household if she could? Still, it was clear that George Howard had never let a woman rule him before.

Patricia frowned. Flattered as she was by the regard of one of the most dashing men in London, she was not about to lose her enjoyment of being admired just to be with him. She had had many beaux and knew she had never remained fond of any one for very long. Yet a man like Lord Ross would be certain to age well. With a gentleman like him attending her, she could not fail to be admired.

Lord Leland was not at all surprised when his wife complained about the business.

"Don't worry," said Lord Leland, "it will all come to nothing. In the first place, I do not think the boy is steady enough not to lose his inheritance at cards before he is out of mourning. He is a good lad, but I doubt if he can give up his cronies as easily as he thinks. If people suppose Patricia is about to marry this young gamecock, it may prompt a certain person to come up to the mark at last."

"Lord Belvidere?" asked his wife. Her eyes softened and her face took on a dreamy look. Beside Lord Belvidere, Ross looked the hardened veteran he was. Belvidere, only a few years younger, but so boyish, so *soigné*, was a perfect gentleman who had already gained distinction as an orator and a poet.

Leland smiled. He knew that Belvidere was too gentle to stand a chance with Patricia. No, she was better matched where she could quarrel. But he thought it best to let his wife think what she liked. It was not worth the effort to say any more.

Lady Leland contented herself with the thought that if necessary, she herself could see to it that the Ross match never took place.

16

Chapter 4

Meanwhile George Howard moved out of his lodgings, paid his debts, and sent word of Edward's death to Mrs. Randall, the housekeeper at the estate. Then he set out for Oakhaven on his favorite horse, Hector. As speed was not important, he meant to have his mount with him for the hunt he was planning.

As he rode out on the turnpike, George looked back to see the smoke of London rising on the morning air, and through it the orange glow of dawn. Ahead in the hedgerows birds were singing, and George felt as light-hearted as he had in Spain, when he marched away to a battle not caring whether or not he returned alive, but taking pleasure in every moment since each might be his last.

On the way, George called at the home of the family solicitor, Mr. Simmons.

"Do sit down, my lord," said Mrs. Simmons putting her embroidery to one side. He started at the realization that she was addressing him. George searched the incredibly cluttered room with his eyes because he had the vague notion that somewhere among the bric-a-brac some other "milord" was lurking.

"I am sorry," went on his hostess, "that Mr. Simmons is keeping you waiting—but his gout has been so terrible lately; he did not finish making ready the papers you must see."

"There is not the least hurry," George assured her, although he contemplated the coming conversation with horror. Mrs. Simmons began by pumping him unmercifully about the circumstances of his brother's death, and George was hard put to it to convince her that the bare facts were indeed all he knew.

"And how did his ward take it?" went on Mrs. Simmons.

"Excuse my ignorance," said George, "but I was not in Edward's confidence. I was not aware that my brother had a ward."

"Of course he had. She is Mr. Hugh Amberly's daughter. Amberly was Alpthorp's fourth son—carried on with ruins, and barrows, and such nonsense, until he died in Italy in 1814."

"Then why is Alpthorp not her guardian?"

Mrs. Simmons quivered in pleasure at being able to recount her story to so distinguished and ignorant a hearer. "Well," she said, "Mr. Hugh Amberly was in the army, and he fell in love with a French girl—not an *emigré* as you may think, but a Jacobin! The girl was well enough, they say. I myself never met her. Lord Alpthorp disapproved so strongly of the connection that he disowned his son. Claire was born in France and bred up in Italy, after her mother died. When she came here, in 'fourteen I think it was, she was telling her beads like a regular papist and would speak naught but Italian! I am sure she must have been a trial to his lordship."

George could only sympathize with any orphan left in the care of so hard and cold a man as his brother Edward. It intrigued him to think he would not be as alone at Oakhaven as he had supposed. The girl could not be out. If she had been presented in London, he would surely have heard of it from Desmarais, who took a ridiculous interest in debutantes.

Mrs. Simmons continued. "I heard nothing about her coming out. She must be eighteen or thereabouts by now, since she has been at Oakhaven four years, and from what I have heard, her governesses have done her precious little good. . . ."

"What does she look like?" interrupted George. A ward was nearly a member of the family.

"She was very thin and shabby when she was here, but I suppose good English food must have made her grow. I did not think her well bred or well conducted, but his lordship said she was half mad with grief. How she can have altered, I do not know." Mrs. Simmons's mouth turned down at the corners in disapproval, as if she were preventing herself by Christian effort from saying something unkind. At that moment Mr. Simmons's heavy step was heard at the top of the stairs. George looked toward the sound, remembering another flight of stairs—at Leland House. Patricia had been so graceful, and her smile so exciting, he did not know how he could bear to wait for her company for even a few more nights.

In the seclusion of the library, Mr. Simmons read Edward's will. To George's surprise it was the same will, made in 1811, that had been in force when he incurred his brother's displeasure. Originally it had annoyed him by its high-handed provision that to inherit he must be married or marry within the year. George was aware that the provision was not meant against him, but against his cousin Michael Howard, who would be next of kin if neither Edward nor his brother were to produce an heir. That this will had never been altered must have been an oversight on Edward's part. George was to receive the entire fortune. The value of the estate was far greater than George had supposed. Two pensions from the government had swelled it hugely, as had the quadrupled rents brought in by the farms during the wartime shortages. Edward had spent almost nothing on the house and grounds, which would have come to George in any case. The will had another proviso, however: To inherit, George had to fulfill all Edward's legal obligations. George had already made up his mind to marry, so that once irksome requirement did not concern him; but among the legal duties to which his brother had been subject was the guardianship of one Claire Amberly.

George protested to Mr. Simmons. "I am quite unfit for the duty, as I am scarcely ten years older than my ward!" he objected.

"Nevertheless, if you do not accept the obligation, your cousin could break the will."

"But surely he must see that a guardian with my sort of reputation can only hurt the child."

"He was here yesterday and insisted that the will be read to him. He had a secretary with him, who took it all down in shorthand. He was surprised, as

19

you were, my lord, that you had not been left out of the fortune, and I fear he has been badly dipped of late. However, although I fear your cousin is angry and means trouble, you have nothing really to worry about. Marry the chit off, and your obligation will be at an end." Having thus disposed of the disappointed Mr. Michael Howard, Mr. Simmons began to discuss the sorry condition of Oakhaven.

As he was taking his leave, it occurred to George to ask whether or not Lord Alpthorp had ever been approached by his brother on Miss Amberly's behalf. Simmons answered, "Yes, he did inquire of Alpthorp, of course. Ross had no desire to keep the child. Things had been so unsettled on the continent, he had Alpthorp send the reply to me. I'll never forget the day they came here, direct from Dover. She was in mourning—a thin brown slip of a girl, but her eyes! Well, my lord, I can only say they were savage." As he spoke, Simmons had turned back into the library and was searching a drawer of his desk. After extracting several old packets and riffling through them, he handed Lord Ross a piece of expensive paper covered with what could only be termed a rude scrawl. George read:

> I am in receipt of yours of the 19th in which you attempt to foist off on me the offspring of a man whose existence I no longer recognize.
>
> Even if you can supply proofs that the foreign papist child now in your custody is indeed an Amberly—and I do not think you can do so—it does not alter the fact that the brat's blood is tainted. As she is the daughter of a Jacobin tart, I do not wish to acknowledge the connection.
>
> I am, etc.
> Alpthorp

Simmons continued, ". . . When we read the letter to his lordship, she was sitting there—in that chair, waiting because she didn't understand a word of English, looking as if she'd seen the devil at the door."

"Perhaps," mused Lord Ross, "she understood more English than you thought."

"Why, no," interposed Mrs. Simmons, who had joined them in the hall, "we couldn't get her to say a word...."

"Now, Melissa," said her husband severely, "we have rattled on long enough. Lord Ross has business to attend to," and with an apologetic flutter Mrs. Simmons saw their visitor out.

George partook of a refreshing meal and a cool glass of cider at the best hotel as he was now a rich man—richer by far than he had thought possible. He felt particularly grateful to Lord Leland for having approved his suit without knowing this. In high spirits he decided to ride for Oakhaven at once.

Chapter 5

Claire Amberly rode into the stable yard, and dismounted with practiced grace, throwing her leg over Virgil's back. It did not perturb her in the slightest that the groom had seen more than he should of her petticoat.

"Miss Claire, must you ride astride like that?" Hawkins asked pettishly. "What would Lord Ross say if 'e was t' see you?"

Claire, who had begun to walk Virgil around, turned and faced the groom with annoyance. "He would say what he pleased!" she retorted.

"I've told you oft enough, miss, a lady don't ride so. It's improper!"

Claire turned back to the horse. "I am no lady," she said in a muffled voice. She had been taxed with this so often that she firmly believed it, but every time she heard it, it hurt a little more.

"If y'ain't a lady, Miss Claire, what are you?" went on Hawkins a little more agreeably, seeing that his scolding had hit the mark. "But I forgot. Missus Randall says y'are to go up t' the house at once. There's a letter she says ye must see, an' she'll be all in a flutter till you've read it."

"Yes, sir," said Claire gravely, "if you will walk my horse."

"That's just what I mean. Ye shouldn't call me 'sir,' and Virgil isn't yer 'orse."

"Yes, he is, because Lord Ross never rides him except when there is a fox hunt!" replied Claire vehemently. "And why shouldn't you be 'sir'? Papa taught me to call all men 'sir.'"

"But I'm not one of yer pa's gen'leman friends," objected Hawkins mildly.

"He would have liked you," Claire said with a smile. "He loved animals, and you have such a way with them. I think you're half animal yourself."

"Get on wi' y', miss," Hawkins grinned, "before I set Twister after you." Twister started barking.

Claire began to run. She knew Hawkins would never get angry, no matter how silly she was! He really is half animal, she thought gloomily. Why is there no one around who is interesting? Claire hoped the letter was from Lord Ross. Indeed, who else would write to them? His letters were the only breaks in the friendlessness of her life, a condition which she would have been the first to admit she had brought on herself.

When Claire arrived in the hall, the house servants were all standing around eyeing the letter, open on the tray. Mrs. Randall, in a great state of agitation, snatched it up and handed it to Claire, who noticed the worry in the housekeeper's habitually imperturbable eyes. "Read," commanded Randall in a choked tone.

The letter was formal notice from George Howard of his brother's death.

Claire was as much taken aback by the servants' reaction to the news as she had been by the news itself. The servants had suffered as much as she from Lord Ross's parsimony, so why were they so affected? Randall had sunk into one of the expensive French chairs.

"Please, Mrs. Randall," she begged, "do not cry." Somehow it was frightening to see the phlegmatic overlord of the house so completely overset.

"He'll throw me out," sobbed Randall. "In heaven's name, what shall I do?"

Claire, scanning the letter, read over the signature again, with its large G and tiny eo, followed by a back-handed L that showed clearly that the writer was left-handed, and in a hurry. George L. Howard . . .

"Do be still," said the cook, Bennett. "George 'oward will do no such thing. He may be bad, but 'e couldn't do that!"

"Who is George Howard?" Claire asked.

23

"Why the poor lamb don't even know! George Howard is the heir—the new Lord Ross, and there's no love lost between us, I can assure you!" ejaculated Randall, blowing her nose.

"Is he the boy in the portrait?" asked Claire, picturing the family group in the salon, with the beautiful Lady Ross and her dark-haired son curled in lazy affection at her feet, his large restless eyes turned outward into the room. Bennett nodded. "But I thought he must be dead." Lord Ross had never so much as mentioned his brother.

" 'e might as well 'ave been for all Lord Ross cared," said Bennett.

"Now that's not true, and you know it," returned Randall. "In 1812, when Mr. George's leg was wounded, Lord Ross had Westgate here to tend him."

"And when Westgate stopped his laudanum, Lord Edward locked Mr. George up and let him shout for it. I'll not forget that day in a 'urry," said Bennett. "After that Mr. George went to London, and there was a scandal there, which was the reason for 'is being cut off."

"What kind of scandal was it?" asked Claire.

"Over a female . . ." began Bennett.

"That is none of Miss Claire's affair," said Randall sharply.

"But if 'e's to be 'er guardian, she should know about 'im," persisted Bennett.

"You goose! Lord Ross would never choose his brother to be Miss Claire's guardian. Why, the man is a known rake, and a gambler in the bargain. He shall gamble away all Lord Edward's money and turn us out to save our keep!" Suddenly Randall began to cry again wildly. She was so severely afflicted with the vapors that Bennett had to ask Ellen to help the housekeeper to her room.

"Could he really be my guardian, Bennett?" asked Claire. "It's likely, I think," said the cook. "Because who would 'ave thought Lord Ross would die before you married? Why, you might 'ave been married in two years time!"

"I don't intend to marry, Bennett," said Claire with finality. She looked quite shaken, and the cook put an

24

arm around her. Bennett felt drawn to the girl, who had no idea, in all her fierce innocence, how lovely she had grown to be. Bennett hoped fervently that George Howard would not neglect Claire as Lord Edward had done. Penniless as she was, Claire's only hope for a decent life was to be married.

"Of course you shall marry," she assured Claire. "You're a right good-looking girl when you tidy yourself up a bit." Claire gave her a scornful look, but Bennett did not even seem to notice. "The thing is," went on the cook, "when Mr. George 'oward, I mean Lord Ross, comes 'ere, you mustn't let yourself be taken with 'im. 'e 'as ruined at least four reputations, so you must be careful not to let it go to your 'ead if 'e shows you attention."

"I do not want attention," said Claire. "I want to be left alone to do as I please."

"You are only eighteen, Miss Claire," said Bennett affectionately, "and 'is lordship is a man of experience. People might suppose it a wonderful opportunity for you to make a good match, but Mr. George 'oward would never marry you, so don't think it!"

"I cannot see what makes you think that I want to marry Lord Ross's brother or any other man." Claire was quite offended.

"I'm sorry, Miss Claire. It's just that if I was a girl without a penny to my name, and a man as 'andsome as George 'oward was to do so much as look at me, I'd be sorely tempted to fall 'opelessly in love with 'im," apologized Bennett.

"Do not mind me," said Claire. "I'm sorry I was cross, but it is provoking not to know. . . ."

"You're right," said Bennett. "It is provoking, but I must do the cooking just the same."

"Would you like me to help you?" asked Claire a little shyly. "I could make a tart for Randall."

"Oh, no, miss. You just shouldn't 'elp me at all, because it ain't right for a lady. What would 'is lordship think if 'e knew we let you do servants' work?"

As Bennett took herself gloomily off to the kitchen, Claire was left with the new resolve that she would never toady to the new Lord Ross because he was handsome or for any other reason. Then she went up to her room in the old stone tower, where she fell into a chair with her current book—the adventures of Gulliver in the land of the Houhynyms. She read on until dinner, without remembering to brush her long tawny hair or pull the burrs off the hem of her skirt.

The following morning Collins arrived at Oakhaven with most of Lord Ross's things, warning the staff that his master would be arriving next day. With Collins came indirect word that the new master might be married very soon. Lord Ross had confided in his valet, and it was not long before Bennett knew the whole story. There was a certain amount of chatter in the servants' hall on the subject, and shabby Miss Amberly, being taken for a servant by the unwitting Collins, was party to it all.

"An earl's daughter! Do you think she will have him?" asked Randall.

"And why should she not?" defended Bennett aggressively. " 'is bad leg won't prevent 'is being a good 'usband."

"What about 'is rovin' eye?" Hawkins asked, and Ellen and Bennett laughed. Claire felt ill. The estate was changing hands and so was she. Although she hated her dull safe life, she feared a new guardian. Perhaps the will would assign her elsewhere, but if it were fool enough to leave her in the care of Edward's rakish brother, there was little she could do about it. Maybe George Howard would send her away to a school or a convent as Edward had sometimes threatened to do. In the heat of her worry Claire forgot that she was really too old for that kind of treatment.

Hawkins, who loved sports of every kind, had enticed Collins to recount George Howard's latest sporting venture—a curricle race between Dover and Brighton. Collins himself had acted as tiger, since it had been decided on the spur of the moment and there was no one else available that George would trust.

" 't wasn't even 'is rig, I 'eard," interrupted Hawkins.

"He rented it," went on Collins. "He said he couldn't

afford to take such risks in his own curricle! Doesn't have a curricle—he has never had a curricle, but he outraced all six of the others. I thought he'd kill us both. I'd not go again. Life's short enough without asking for the undertaker."

" 'ow much did 'e win?"

"Two thousand pounds, and it was not a penny too much. It was all gone in a week."

Claire told herself it was disgusting that Oakhaven was to go to a careless fool. To spend two thousand pounds in a week could only be the completest folly. She resolved not to be there when George Howard arrived, and if that made him angry with her, perhaps he would send her away and end the boredom and isolation that were driving her mad. She would even speak rudely to him. A guardian who disliked her would be nothing new, and any change might be for the better.

Chapter 6

The sun was warm and a gentle breeze ruffled the dry grass. After a short while George left the turnpike and struck out across the fields. Riding across country could save time if the hedges had not grown too thick.

George looked around him as he rode, and his pleasure in his exercise was marred by the poverty he saw all about him. Five years ago there had been more cows and fewer ragged children. The trees had not been pollarded yet for firewood, and game had been more abundant. The nearer he came to Oakhaven, the worse things seemed to be.

He was no more than an hour from the edge of the estate when George saw a female rider approaching from the far side of the field. He thought she must be a farmer's daughter because she was riding astride and appeared rather shabby. Yet, there was something aristocratic about the graceful flow of her long tawny curls, and something distinctly aristocratic about her horse, which was one of the most magnificent George had seen. Desiring to discover more about this lady (if lady she was) who dared to venture out without escort or the decency of a bonnet to cover her flagrant hair, George altered his course to intercept hers. Immediately she swerved and reversed direction. She tossed her hair and looked askance at him as if daring him to follow. George speeded his horse a trifle, not being one to turn back from adventure. The lass spurred her mount to a gallop, with George still behind her, too exhilarated to remember his manners.

Then a high hedge, too thick for the horses to squeeze through, loomed up before them. George reined in his mount a little, feeling sure that his quarry would do the same—but much to his astonishment her horse sailed over it with awesome ease. It was all George could do to keep Hector from refusing, but he had to follow. Now his curiosity was really piqued. The girl's mount was one of the finest jumpers in his experience, and she rode him superbly.

After clearing the hedge rather clumsily, Hector got his wind up and showed the speed for which he was renowned, overtaking the girl within a quarter of a mile. Matching his speed to hers, he rode beside her for a few minutes, and when at last she saw that she could not outdistance him, she slowed her horse to a walk.

"That's a fine stallion you have," he said, smiling into her frightened eyes. They were a gray so dark as to be almost black.

"Yes, sir," she said warily.

"What is his name?" asked George. He knew that girls' names for their horses are often keys to their feelings.

"I call him Virgil," she answered, looking away shyly and patting the stallion's mane.

"Why do you call him that?" George was surprised to hear a classical allusion in such a rustic setting.

She thought for a moment before turning her head to answer gravely, "He has been my guide through all the outer rings of hell." She looked at her pursuer again, a little less cautiously. He was certainly very handsome, with his unruly dark hair fallen over one eye. On his cheek was a scar made by a saber cut, but its presence did not make him look fierce or wicked.

George would not make unwelcome advances to any girl, but would his advances really be unwelcome? Bringing Hector a little closer, he noticed that the lass was tensed to flee, her knuckles turning white across the handle of her crop. He was used to reading such small signs and stopped approaching, but he was already very near. "I thought all the hells were in London," he said.

Then the girl turned to him impulsively and asked, "Have you ever made Mr. George Howard's ac-

29

quaintance?" The man spoke of London and of gambling hells—perhaps he knew the new master of Oakhaven.

Suddenly George realized that he was in the presence of his ward and with difficulty he suppressed the laugh that welled up inside him. He put his head down slightly to hide the effort.

"Yes, miss. I have," he answered.

"Can you tell me what manner of gentleman he is? I know I should not be inquisitive, but he is coming to see us today, and so I should like to know." Her face looked drawn with worry.

"Why, what have you heard about this Mr. George Howard?"

"I have heard that he is a gambler." She said it boldly but without condemnation.

"He may be a gambler, but he is also a man of honor. I like him exceedingly." George's merriment spread itself across his face in an irrepressible grin. Claire felt suddenly frightened, wheeled about, and rode away from him into a wood.

George laughed freely as soon as she was out of earshot. The joke was on him now, but wait until they were formally introduced! It was a pity she had turned out to be his ward . . . but nothing he had heard had led him to expect a beauty. That hair and those grave, lovely eyes were irresistible. If only her clothes were not so atrocious! George frowned. It was criminal the way his brother had neglected the estate and the girl as well. If she were my daughter, I would discipline her, he thought grimly . . . but if she were my child, I'd have made sure she was well dressed, carefully chaperoned and, of course, brought out. Still, George could not help but feel Claire had behaved as if she knew her conduct was dangerous. Even so, it was not often that she could meet an opponent as swiftly mounted as he, and she had not been wanton or even uncivil. In fact nothing would have happened if it had not been for his own bad manners.

George rode around his estate to observe its condition, a labor that took some time because he stopped often to speak to his tenants. When at last he arrived at Oakhaven, his mind was filled with the work that lay ahead to set things right.

The house was equally in poor repair, and George's first instruction to Randall, who appeared before him with inner trembling, was to hire a butler and two maids at once, plus a lad to help Hawkins in the stable. From that time the housekeeper refused to hear a word against him, even from Bennett.

George then asked Randall if he might speak to Claire's governess and was surprised to learn that the chit had been totally unsupervised for over half a year.

"She has had five different ones, my lord," said Randall.

"Is she so difficult, then?"

"Well, no, my lord, but I think she was too clever for them."

"Indeed. Where is Miss Claire now?" At this question Randall became flustered.

"Perhaps she is visiting one of the cottagers," replied the housekeeper uncertainly. "I will tell her when she returns that you wish to see her."

"Had you not told her I was coming today and that she should be here?"

"Yes, my lord. She said it would not matter to you and she did not have to obey me."

"That will do, Randall," said George. As the object of his childhood pranks politely withdrew, George went into the library to look through his brother's papers and remained engrossed in them until dinnertime. Bennett announced dinner later than usual, but George did not notice, used as he was to London hours. Miss Claire had still not appeared, and the big dining hall seemed dimmer for being empty. A chill wind had begun to blow and the draft made George's bad knee ache. He had not bothered to change into evening dress, although Collins had brought his things down from London by coach, Lord Ross sat down to the table with his boots on. Bennett had outdone herself; the food was delicious, and George realized how much he had missed Bennett, his father

31

and mother, and even Edward—in fact how much he had missed having a family to love and care for him. With Patricia Leland he could create a family of his own here at Oakhaven, but she would despise the drafty discomfort of the place. He must invite her as soon as possible and enlist her help and good taste in making Oakhaven livable. Then perhaps Lady Patricia would not be so set against living at least part of the year in the country. A good landlord does not live away all the time.

George stood up, called Bennett to him, and complimented her on the excellence of the meal. She said, "It was just plain country food, my lord."

"No, 'my lords,' for you, Bennett. Couldn't you still call me 'George'?"

"Oh, I couldn't, my lord," she said, blushing deeply.

Then George went back to the library, but too tired to work any longer, he sat down in a chair near the fire, with his bad leg up to get the weight off it. Although he could now walk and even dance so well that no one could tell at first that he had an injury, the knee hurt a little all the time and was usually worse when he had danced on it.

George poured himself a glass of brandy and sat thinking in the gathering darkness. It occurred to him that perhaps the reason Claire had failed to come home was because she was afraid of him. She had not known him during their encounter, that was certain. Perhaps she had heard of his reputation for wildness or, on the other hand, perhaps she expected him to be like Edward. It was in this very room that Edward Howard, as his guardian, had called George to account for numerous sins. Now he was on the other side of the desk. No matter how many excuses he was able to find for his ward, it still annoyed him to be kept waiting. He had always hated to wait, and because he did not know Claire, he worried a little about her safety, although he doubted she could still be in the woods at this hour.

At that moment Claire Amberly was brushing the straw from her hair and leaving the abandoned barn where she often hid. Within a few minutes, she had ridden to the house and gone to change her clothes.

A remarkably short time after the muffled sounds of her entrance into the hallway had died away, George heard footsteps in the corridor. The room was now quite dark, as candles had not been brought in. Only a pale light from the rising moon and a warmer glow from the coals on the hearth limned the objects in that familiar space. George swung his bad leg stiffly to a more dignified position. The door opened and Claire Amberly, dressed in a neat blue frock that was sadly out of the fashion, came into the room bearing a candelabrum. Its light made her hair seem as bright as flame, but she could not see his face beyond its sphere. Mrs. Randall, standing behind her, made the introduction and withdrew.

George made his voice sound deep and strange. "Why were you so late in arriving, Miss Amberly?"

She advanced slowly toward the desk. "I lost my way, sir," she said vaguely.

"That is most arrant nonsense, miss," he retorted, this time without bothering to disguise his voice. "You know those woods like the back of your hand!"

Claire put the candelabrum down at last and saw the same gentleman who had chased her that afternoon. Her eyes widened and her lips parted, but she made no sound.

"Mephistopheles, at your service," said George lazily.

"I'm sorry, sir," said Claire. "It seems I did not know who I was inconveniencing."

"You knew very well you were inconveniencing Mr. George Howard. What you did not know was the name of your flirt," he answered.

"Did you know me?" she asked, a bit shakily.

"After you mentioned my name, yes. And it was all that saved you from being thoroughly kissed! Do you always ride astride?"

"No, sir. I do it when I think I will be unobserved," she answered, without the slightest contrition in her tone, and continued rudely, "Do you always chase girls?"

"Of course," George replied, "as you have no doubt

33

heard, it is my invariable custom, but I do not often encounter one who rides astride."

Reluctantly, Claire smiled. "How would you like it if you had to ride sidesaddle, sir?" she retorted.

George imagined himself on a sidesaddle and laughed. Then he fixed her with a stare that was neither amused nor amusing. Claire met his relentless blue eyes for as long as she dared. At last she looked away.

"Why on earth," inquired his lordship, "did you want to be rude to me?" For a long time Claire did not dare to answer. "Tell the truth, and I will not be angry," he told her.

Claire did not look up. "I wanted you to send me away," she whispered.

"But why?"

"Because I loathe living here. The people in the neighborhood all despise me, except Bennett. There is no one to talk to and I have read nearly all the books, except the Greek. . . . You could refuse to be my guardian. I could go back to Italy. I could go out and work!"

"Could you teach French and the pianoforte?" asked George, faintly amused now that he thought he understood.

"No, sir." He noticed her additional rudeness in not giving him his brother's title, but did not hold it against her, as he did not quite like "my lord" yet.

"Are you perfectly respectable? Can you give references?"

"No, sir, but I know history and mathematics, Latin, Italian, and enough French to get along pretty well."

"Unfortunately no one is going to hire you as a tutor," said her guardian dryly. "You would constitute far too big a temptation to the boys."

"But you should send me away," insisted the girl, sticking to her original plan, although by now she no longer thought it a good one. George could see that she was ashamed and was sorry for her, but did not say so. On the contrary he addressed her sternly.

"I cannot send you away. My brother's will has designated me your guardian. The thing I must do is take you in hand. You will not ride Virgil or any other horse astride from this out. If you deliberately disobey me, I will make you sorry for it, Miss Amberly."

If Claire had been able to speak what she felt, she would have said she was sorry already, but she could say nothing. George's eyes were too much for her. George saw that she could not answer and took pity on her.

"You may go now—upstairs, to your room." When Claire had gone, George felt no satisfaction at having taught his ward a lesson. He was only sorry that he had to deny himself the pleasure of teaching her a lesson of a very different kind. She had spoken of the outer rings of hell, which Dante had traversed in the *Inferno*, with Virgil's help. If Oakhaven had been a hell to her, its innermost frozen ring must be the room to which she had just been sent. George resolved that he would make it his business to see that she would not regard it so in the future. Claire had been deliberately rude to him, but had seemed so vulnerable. She had courage and ready wit. It was his duty as her guardian to see that she learned enough manners to turn them to advantage.

Up in her room Claire sat for a long time on a straight chair, thinking furiously. She had certainly been mistaken about Mr. George Howard! He had not been at all like Lord Edward and was not nearly as old as she had supposed. No wonder he looked like such a child in the portrait! He had not arrived by post, as his brother always did. He had not changed for dinner, and most unbelievable of all, he was not wearing any sign of mourning! Claire was angry with herself for not having realized who he was just the same. Now she had put her first foot wrong as usual, and he would never like her. It was maddening to have been so mistaken.

Claire picked up her hairbrush and began to use it vigorously. Sparks flew off her hair and disappeared instantly into the darkness. She was hungry but did not dare to go downstairs. She had been sent to her room. If Lord Edward had caught her in such behav-

35

ior, she would surely have been punished much more severely.

Claire put on her nightgown and lay in bed with her eyes wide open, thinking about how George Howard had laughed at her.

Chapter 7

The next morning, when George went down to the stable for his ride, he found Claire, in a badly patched dress, currying Virgil. It piqued him to see her doing servants' work.

"What are you doing?" he said sharply.

She turned, startled, and it was several seconds before she realized who had spoken to her and why. "I always do this, sir. Hawkins doesn't have time." Apologetically she took up the comb again. "His lordship wanted me to take good care of him." There she was again, speaking as if Edward were still alive.

"Did you like my brother?" George asked her.

"No, sir, but I respected him," she answered, looking at George cautiously out of the corner of her dusky, long-lashed eyes.

But you do not respect me, he thought. How could you? Immediately she sensed that something was wrong. She would never understand George Howard, and she could never please him.

"Sir Edward disapproved of me also," she said.

"It was cruel of Edward to let you grow up living like a servant."

Claire drew herself up bravely. "I do *not* live like a servant. I work only when I please."

"So you like carrying candles and currying horses."

"And I hate to cut out dresses. That is why my skirts are patched," she said defiantly.

Abandoning his plan to ride before breakfast, George went up to the house with Claire, who became totally absorbed in muffins with cream cheese and currant jelly.

"We only get things like these when someone is here," she observed.

"Then someone had better be here more often, Miss Claire," he replied, taking another bite of bacon, "and if you are not to disgrace me before company, you must have new clothes. After breakfast we will drive to the village seamstress and choose some patterns."

Claire hated fittings. She hated holding still, posing obediently, being measured, manipulated, fussed over, and pricked with pins. She hated Mrs. Arbuthnot, the seamstress, who always called her my *dear* Miss Amberly, and who smelled strongly of musk. And most of all Claire hated her own image in the fitting-room glass because it showed every flaw, every awkwardness.

"No, thank you," she told him. "I did not mean to make you think I am not satisfied. I only wear my old skirts to ride, because it keeps the good ones from getting dirty. I have much better frocks upstairs."

"Then go up," he said implacably, "and put one on, because you are going to do as I say."

Claire complied and was driven to the village in Edward's old phaeton. George's offer to let her take the reins went unaccepted and did not even produce a smile. George was annoyed at her sullen ingratitude and felt it distinctly odd that she did not share the general feminine passion for clothes. They pulled up outside Mrs. Arbuthnot's shop and he frowned down at her.

"If I ask you aught while we are inside, you are to give me prompt and truthful answers. Is that clear?"

"Yes, my lord." The sound of her answer came as a shock. At last she had said it. Perhaps his efforts to please her had not been as vain as he thought.

Mrs. Arbuthnot showed hundreds of drawings to George. His first selection was a riding habit in the latest fashion. Mrs. Arbuthnot showed him a number of swatches of fabric. "Which of these colors would you prefer, Miss Claire?" asked her guardian.

"I would prefer black, my lord."

Lord Ross gave her a hard look. Black was hardly appropriate for a young girl . . . but on second thought he decided it would become her. Black for the habit was chosen. Next he ordered four dresses, rejecting anything elaborate, but choosing the most expensive goods. Then he left Claire to be measured while he met with a few of his tenants to discuss their rents.

After the tenants' meeting, Lord Ross called at Mrs. Arbuthnot's to collect his ward. As she climbed up onto the seat of the phaeton she grumbled, "I feel like a pincushion," but she did not seem as sullen as before. They rode on for about a mile in silence, without even looking at each other. Then Claire said, "I am sorry I was rude to you last night. It just seemed awful to change hands like . . . like an uncollectable marker for a hundred pounds!" George laughed. He knew circles where a female of her quality would bring a great deal more than that. "Why do you have to laugh at me?" she asked bitterly.

"I was not laughing at you, but at my own stupid thoughts; and you are not really changing hands, because you are still a member of the Howard household—more so than I have been myself. It's almost as if you were one of my family, but I know so little about you, Claire. You should feel it your duty to enlighten me."

She noticed that he had gone from calling her Miss Amberly to Miss Claire and then to Claire in the space of one day, which was not at all proper of him. "I'm very bad at knowing my duty, my lord," she answered.

"Why did you choose black for your habit?" he persisted.

"Because of Papa." George could see that the mere mention of her father made her sad, and he thought of the time when his own parents had been alive.

"He must have been a fine man, for you to mourn him so long," said George.

"Everybody around here despises him because he died poor," she said fiercely. "They say he was a worthless wastrel but he was not. He took very good care of me. That is why I walked out of Mrs. Reynolds's dinner party—because she said Papa was no good."

"Maybe you should not have let it bother you."

"Would you have let people say things like that about your father?"

George had to admit he would not. "What was it

39

like in Italy?" he asked her. "Who stayed with you, and where did you play?"

Then Claire found herself telling George all about her father and their life together—things she hadn't told before to anyone—because telling would have made her feel the loss all over again. They talked all the way up to the house, through luncheon, and afterward, until the vicar came to call. Then Claire went up to her room, where as soon as she was alone, she realized she had told her guardian far too much. She had said things she had never mentioned to Lord Edward or Bennett or even Beaugency. It had been almost worth it, but now he knew enough to make him despise her absolutely. She had never been and never would be respectable. Furthermore, George Howard now knew how she hated the world of lords and ladies who had thrown her father out, and it was simple logic that since he was a baron, he was included in that world. Claire told herself that it did not matter if George Howard went back to London knowing how she hated the peerage, because after he left things would return to the way they had been before. Except that she would never forget his eyes.

However, to Claire's surprise, Lord Ross did not go back to town that week, as his brother would certainly have done. It did not take him long to entirely overset the house with the work he put in hand. Before long there were over sixty people at work on the estate, trimming the overgrown hedges, cutting the furze he had given the cottagers for winter fuel, and repairing the buildings.

The unused portion of the stables was being cleaned out, and the roof of the west wing was being noisily furnished with new slates and gutters. From her high window in the north tower, Claire could see what went on on the roof, and not all of it was work. The view was interesting if no longer private. People were everywhere in the house as well, cleaning, polishing, and setting things to rights. With the exception of Mr. Jarvis, the new secretary, they were rough working men.

Claire's life was totally changed, but at least she was busy. Besides riding, she now saw the dancing master twice a week, and besides that, she had begun the study of Greek with Mr. Jarvis, using George's smudgy old primer. Randall disapproved of it, but George preferred to indulge Claire in her desire to study the people who had so interested her father. It seemed ironic to him that the artifacts that had fascinated Hugh Amberly, in search for which he had given his life, were now suddenly in fashion. Items Claire's father could not give away during his lifetime were now bringing prices in London that would have made him a rich man.

Claire had fittings to go to, visits from tenant farmers, and all manner of odd things that came up on the spur of the moment. Lord Ross was busy as well, and apart from morning rides and a chess game or two, Claire saw little of him. Most of the time he spent supervising the work on the estate. He had proposed a pact with his tenants, who had protested with some reason that their rents were more than they could pay. The pact offered to reduce rents on condition that wages were raised, to offer the laborers enough to live on. Since the money awarded in relief of poverty came from the parish, higher wages would also largely reduce the necessity for large contributions on Lord Ross's part.

At the same time George declared war on the rabbits, which had proliferated in Edward's absence, overrunning the fields. He gave his laborers permission to come onto the estate and trap or shoot as many of them as they wished for their tables. This was a very welcome suggestion, as many families had been so reduced that they had not been able to afford meat.

One afternoon, when Jarvis had been sent to Bath with a message for the solicitor, George called Claire down to the library to make a fair copy of a letter he had written. It had to be sent in a hurry and his own handwriting was, as he put it, "no damn good." While she was working on it, one of the tenants was announced. He was a beefy individual, expensively dressed, but in very poor taste. The collar of his blue coat was much too high. He argued against Lord Ross's proposal for increasing laborers' wages, and exhibited the most callous indifference to the troubles of his workmen, which he claimed were principally caused by an excess of strong drink. He partook of wine and sandwiches, and continued to insist that Lord Ross abandon the pact, but Lord Ross was adamant. The tenants would sign the pact or be refused lower rents, and that was final.

Then the farmer attacked George for allowing his laborers to hunt rabbits on the estate, claiming that it was bad for their character to be encouraged to engage in poaching, which was usually punished severely by the law. His remarks made Claire so angry that her hand shook, making an unsightly blot on the page. She stood up unexpectedly and said, "Would it be good for your character to have nothing to eat but potatoes and bread?"

This uncalled for piece of rudeness caused the tenant to leave Oakhaven in a huff. Lord Ross was angry.

"Now suppose he does not sign the agreement out of pique because you did not allow him to speak his mind on a matter he is powerless to change? Then his laborers may continue to go hungry because you had to meddle!" He stalked out of the room, leaving her to recopy the letter with nothing to mar her solitude but the distant sounds of hammering drifting in from outdoors. Claire bit back her tears. George had been right. He cared about the laborers as much as she did. If he came back into the room, he must not see her cry.

George knew that Claire would be made unhappy by his hard words, but she certainly deserved them. She never knew when to speak up or when to be silent, and if she were to be married or even come out in society at all, she would have to learn. She was also very stubborn. Repeated warnings and even threats had not kept her from going out into the fields and woods alone—for what reason nobody knew—but so far she had avoided trouble of any kind. At last George had extracted her promise not to ride out alone, and as far as he knew she had kept it.

The next day Claire's riding habit was delivered and she put it on. George did not hide the fact that he admired her in it. After she had mounted Virgil on the sidesaddle, which she still detested, he said to her, "Your father is dead, and so is the little girl you once were. If you have to wear mourning, wear it for her."

Chapter 8

Lady Patricia sighed and composed herself on her gilt chair, waiting for the fourth applicant for the position of lady's maid to Claire Amberly to present herself. She had not supposed it could be so tedious to engage a maid. The last three girls had been hopeless. The first could not speak decent English, the second was untidy (she knew Lord Ross would never stand for that) and the third had been far too stupid to carry out the instructions she was to receive—instructions that involved writing letters.

The month her father had specified could not be up too soon. Soon she could visit Lord Ross, and he her. He had called to see her twice on his visits to town, and he had never seemed more healthy, more devil-may-care, more delighted to sample with her the pleasures of the moment. On his last visit he had taken her out in the new coach that had just been delivered. It was black enamel outside, with no decoration but a thin blue stripe and the Ross coat of arms on the door. Inside it was varnished cherry wood and navy velvet. "It is as sinister as you are," she had told him.

He had replied, "But think how it sets you off!" It would set her off well enough, but what she really wanted was her own phaeton and matched pair of white horses. They would have to be white. . . .

Lord Ross was thrilling company when he was in spirits, but she would almost rather have had him endure her absence less well. Not that she had been pining away for him, though. Colin Quartermayne, Viscount Allenvale, had taken her riding in the park that morning. The evening before she had attended the opera with Lord Belvidere, and that odious

Squire Strathmore had made her an offer at Lady Jersey's ball, although that hardly counted.

At last the housemaid knocked on the door and a dark, petite girl of about seventeen was ushered in. She introduced herself as Bettina Renzo. A brief conversation determined that the girl knew English well enough, and she had brought a sample of her writing. Although the girl's grammar was atrocious and her spelling worse, Lady Patricia was satisfied that they would do for her purposes. Certainly the girl was attractive enough. The one thing that worried Patricia a little was Bettina's youth. Perhaps she would be insufficiently discreet, particularly if she were to become fond of her mistress. Lady Patricia hoped that could be taken care of by establishing the girl's interest directly. She could see that the child was impressed at being interviewed by such a fine lady. Her eyes were cast down modestly.

"Look at me, Bettina," she commanded. Bettina raised her eyes to a vision of style in pale pink. Lady Patricia Leland was fingering a nosegay of tea roses that Colin Quartermayne had given her.

"Would you be willing to work in the country?" she asked.

"Would I be working for yóu, madam?" inquired Bettina.

"No. For a Miss Amberly. Her guardian, Lord Ross, would pay you the usual salary. However, you would also be working for me, because I require to receive news of that household frequently—twice a week if nothing important occurs. I should pay you generously for doing this, and if there are any other services I would require, I should let you know by letter."

"What sort of household news are you interested in, madam?" asked Bettina, coming straight to the point. Patricia was encouraged at her quickness. This girl might do rather well.

"I wish to know who Lord Ross's visitors are. In particular I wish to know the name of any female who is a frequent visitor or who is visited by him. I would like to be informed of Miss Amberly's character—to know what manner of girl she is, and whether or not her guardian has a *tendre* for her.

45

"What is a *'tendre,'* madam?"

"I want to know whether they hold each other in affection. Do you wish to accept the position?"

"Yes, my lady. I'll try to give satisfaction."

"I am sure you will." Lady Patricia treated her new employee to a dazzling smile, and tossing her bouquet to one side, she reached for the bell to ring for the housemaid.

Claire was a bit taken aback by the arrival of her lady's maid. She was torn between her delight at the girl's ability to speak Italian and awe at the attention shown her by the famous Lady Patricia. Claire disliked having her privacy intruded upon, but admittedly the girl's work did save her time and spare her the contortions she used to have to go through to button up the new frocks. In fact the blue one, which was such an odd shade (a sort of dusky heliotrope), was the only one she could remove with ease alone.

However, after a week's time it became obvious to Claire that her abigail had an extremely commonplace mind, her interests ranging from clothing to men, and back again. Claire could have told Bettina to cease her mindless chatter, but she did not feel called upon to do so. Instead she merely stopped listening to it. It was not surprising that the maid was attuned to matters that were central to her trade, and in any case George would have been annoyed if his ward had been able to find a kindred soul in a servant.

Bettina did very well as a lady's maid, although at first she had little to do.

"If she had more duties, she would not have time to listen at keyholes," George said sharply to Mrs. Randall. He had caught the girl listening outside the library door to his conversation with Lady Reynolds about fishing rights in the stream between the two estates.

The outraged Randall had locked Bettina in a closet and offered to give her a whipping, but Claire would not hear of it. "Did Lord Ross tell you to lock her in there?" Claire demanded.

"I can't tolerate snooping in the master's affairs, miss," retorted Randall.

"She is my servant and I demand that you let her out at once!" said Claire imperiously. "She probably did it because she was bored, as anyone of sensibility would be in this place. I will see to it that she does not do it again."

"Very well, miss," said Randall, pressing her lips together in severe disapproval.

Up in her garret room that night Bettina cried a little and wondered if the advancement she expected from this place was worth it. The worst was that she had come to like her young mistress, who, although she was a bit awkward, was certainly a fast learner. Surely Miss Amberly could not have been kinder to her over the business. It was of course possible that Miss Amberly had helped her escape punishment only to annoy Lord Ross.

Bettina had observed the baron and his ward together as closely as she could, and she saw little rancor in the frequent tiffs and reprimands that marked their daily life. She supposed her master must be somewhat fond of the girl, and wrote as much to London. Bettina's report was not flattering to Claire, as the maid undervalued her mistress's talents and was ill equipped to appreciate her wit. However, the letters, ostensibly to Lady Patricia's maid, Anne, let Patricia know that Lord Ross took a much more particular interest in Miss Amberly than was necessary in a guardian.

I wonder if he is taking advantage of her? mused Patricia. Unlikely. After all, George Howard is an honorable man. What is more probable is that the chit is taking advantage of her position to impose on him. The corners of Patricia's mouth turned down in a wry smile. It was not a fleshly liaison, apparently, that was keeping her suitor in the country, but another sort of interest entirely. It was not surprising that Lord Ross should be susceptible to the charms of a healthy, if unaccomplished, young girl, but that such an interest could survive the company of ton people was unthinkable. Lady Patricia had only to acquiesce to Lord Ross's request that she take part in the house party at his estate, and George's interest in his ward would swiftly end. It was too bad. Country house parties were tedious, and her father would insist that her brother Gerald go down as chaperon, and his insufferably insipid wife, Marianne, as well. There was nothing Patricia could do to avoid that, but perhaps there would be other diverting guests.

Chapter 9

It was unseasonably hot, and George Howard was relaxing in his shirt sleeves after a morning of hard work. He stared at the chess pieces on the board before him and rubbed his bad knee absently.

"You have beaten me again, Claire," he said.

His ward gazed gravely across the board at him. "You didn't try, my lord," she answered.

"I certainly did. Do you think I would insult you by letting you win?" He glanced up to meet her dark gray eyes. She was wearing the lightest one of her new frocks and her hair was tied neatly back with a piece of blue ribbon. George realized that he had not tried to get the better of her as hard as he might. "I wish you would call me George," he confided.

Claire smiled at him and shook her head. It would be wrong to call her guardian by his first name. "You always win when we play piquet," she said.

He answered with a touch of impatience, "Piquet was once my living, Claire. You are all that is left of my family. That is why I ask you to call me George."

Claire blushed. George meant what he said. He really did want someone to call him George. Embarrassed, she toyed with the pages of the large book he had brought her from London. It was full of engravings of Italian gardens. "Would you like a rematch, G-George?" she stammered.

"No, thank you. I think I had better take some lessons before we play again, Claire." He said this with such a shy smile that she realized her refusal could have hurt him. It gave her an odd sinking feeling to know she could do this, and she was relieved when he got up and took himself off to oversee the roof repairs.

Claire watched George through the hall window as he climbed the long ladder to the roof of the Tudor hall. She was glad that Hawkins was there to hold the ladder for him. George climbed slowly and deliberately. Halfway up he turned and looked down. Then his gaze swung around the courtyard and he saw her standing in the window. It struck her as odd that he had asked her to call him George, and particularly so because the request had come at the end of a long string of reprimands. Lord Edward had been cold and distracted, but he had never expected much of her. He had offered her so little notice that she had often been able to do as she pleased. With George it was another matter. Claire had been set down for allowing Bettina to listen to his guests' conversation, for failing to fix her hair, for spending time in the servants' hall, and for trying to avoid the dancing master. Each time George had fixed her with his shattering blue eyes and spoken his mind—but the only time he had really seemed angry was when she had ridden out alone. He had made her promise not to do it again, which struck her as grossly unfair, as she could not very well take Hawkins or Bob to her secret place.

Then, as she watched George walk out on the rooftop, with the hot sun glowing white off his broad shoulders, it struck her that although she had promised him not to ride out alone she had never promised not to walk. . . .

Up on the roof George wiped the sweat off his brow with his handkerchief. If Hawkins and Claire had not been there, I would have gone back down, he told himself. He had not been on a ladder since the Battle of Badajoz, when his had been thrown off the battlements by the enemy and he had lain all day under the ladder with his leg broken and three corpses on top of it.

Claire Amberly put on an old apron over her frock and set out quietly for her particular path through the woods. It took her longer to walk the distance than to ride it, but it was the same comforting way she had always gone. She followed a narrow overgrown path that led to a ruined chapel at the edge of the wood. This chapel, whose roofless Roman nave was still standing, was one of her most secret retreats and the site of a labor that, although of no conceivable use, both relaxed and absorbed her. If Claire's father could have seen the care with which his daughter proceeded, he would have thought her a credit to him. She had been engaged for some time in unearthing and assembling a window of gothic glass, which depicted a king surrounded by animals and flowers. The slow discovery of the window's design was a source of challenge, frustration, and sudden joy when she knew a piece was fitted right.

Today the girl stared down at her work restlessly. The king was nearly pieced together, although a large portion of his robe was missing. A ruby crown sat jauntily on his head and an affable deer lay gracefully at his feet. Suddenly Claire noticed that his eyes had the same shy, amused expression George's often had when he questioned her. Damn the man, she thought. He has even followed me here. Claire stood up and put distance between her and the elegant painted smile. No. The face wasn't sneering. She had to admit that George did not really sneer at her either. It would be easier to be angry with him if he did. It was just that George was always sure, so damnably sure he was right! "King George," she whispered to herself, "I hate you." She picked up the pale amber fragment with its tiny charming face, closed her fist over it briefly, and replaced it as before. Then she set to work.

Late in the afternoon it became colder. Clouds covered the lowering sun and a breeze came up, riffling through the purple asters. Claire covered her work with dry leaves as usual and set off for home. As she walked along the path, the sky became darker and the wind gustier, whipping little branches across her path. When she had walked about halfway to Oakhaven, she entered a part of the woods so dense that during the summer she could wait out rain squalls in its shade. On the path ahead she could see two men standing in the shadows. One of them was carrying a sack. Immediately she suspected that they had poached birds, and if they were strangers it was possible that they might offer her violence. In spite of her dirty apron, she was too well dressed to pass as a farm girl. Claire almost turned on her heel to run, but she saw little advantage in it. Instead she kept briskly on down the path until she could see their faces and was relieved to find they were both young men she knew.

"Hallo, Jemmy. Hallo Dick," she said politely.

"Good day to you, Miss Amberly," said Jemmy, looking shyly at the ground, as she passed on down the path. Then she heard footsteps following her, and turning, found herself facing the large slender frame of Dick Morgan.

"Miss Amberly, ye'll not be tellin' the young lord ye saw us here?" He looked as if he would like to lay hands on her but she did not move.

"What would I want to do that for? Your mother has enough to worry about without you in prison!" she said with an arrogance she did not feel. Claire turned her back on them and continued primly down the path until they were well out of sight. Then she began to run. Her blue ribbon caught on a twig and was torn from her hair but she did not notice. The rain that had threatened fell in small ragged showers and then stopped again. Claire's skirts began to cling to her legs. She hitched them up and continued to hurry; her familiar woods no longer felt quite so safe. As she came up the hill behind Oakhaven, she suddenly saw Lord Ross on horseback. She realized that he must have come looking for her. As he reined in, Hector reared, and Claire stepped back so rapidly she nearly fell.

George's lips were slightly parted, and his hair had fallen across his forehead.

"You are late," he said.

"I'm sorry," she answered. "My walk took me longer than I thought."

George dismounted "Where have you been, Claire?" he asked. "You are out of breath—running from somewhere." Claire realized that her hair was

52

blowing about her face in wild disarray and that she was short of breath.

"I was running because I knew I was late, George." She threw his name out boldly. "I knew you were busy and did not think you would miss me." Her eyes would not meet his. She was ashamed that she had to be evasive, but if he knew what she had been doing, he would think it was very childish, or maybe even sacrilegious.

"Where were you?" he insisted.

"When you were young," she countered, "didn't you have somewhere you went to be alone?"

George was stopped for a moment by the idea that to her he was no longer young, but he did not intend to let this thought deflect his inquiry. Perhaps Claire had gone into the woods merely to be alone and perhaps she had not.

"When you gave me your word not to ride out alone, what reasons do you suppose I had to ask for it?" he said, using her own tactic of answering with a question.

Claire thought for a moment. Lord Ross stared gravely down at her, his gloved hand on his hip. He was still angry, but not so much as a few moments before. She did not dare to answer him rudely. "I suppose it was because you were concerned for my safety. . . ."

"Are you safer on Virgil's back or on foot?" he interrupted.

"On Virgil's back, but I gave my word. I am sorry if it caused you worry, George. I was not really in any danger."

"You knew that I consider these woods unsafe. Suppose you met poachers?"

"I did meet poachers." George looked into her eyes and saw that she was in earnest. She had met poachers and dealt with them in such a way as to cause her little worry. In truth, Claire was a female of unusual resource.

"Indeed," was all he said as he turned away from her toward the house. He could see that she had no intention of telling him where she had been, and

53

since her manner indicated that her journey had been an innocent one, he decided not to argue it further.

They ate supper in silence, in a tiny pool of light in the center of the great room, and when he told her of the house party he had planned for the following week, he was surprised to see the color drain from her face. Claire Amberly sat very still, listening to her guardian say that there were to be dinner parties, a ball, and a fox hunt.

"Please, George, let me stay upstairs," she whispered. "You could tell them I am away."

"No, Claire. You will not get off that easily. You may not disappear without permission while my guests are here. You must come down and be polite."

"They will have heard about me," she objected.

"Nonsense. You are too young to have a reputation."

"I made Robbie Hartley break his leg. Everybody knows about it."

"In the county. These are ton people, and I will be ashamed of you if you hide from them. Do not be afraid of your past. Mine is a lot worse than yours, you know," he smiled at her softly. In the candlelight the line of his scar stood out sharply against his cheek. "I just want you to try to like them."

"I cannot promise to like them," said Claire bravely, "but I promise to try to be civil."

When his ward had gone upstairs, George told himself that he was lucky she had promised him anything. She was too independent, he knew, but he could not help liking her that way. It was very important for Claire to "take" with Lady Patricia and her friends, for after all, he must marry within the year. Then, if Claire were to be married in her turn, she would first have to be launched in society by Lady Ross. If Patricia were to give Claire a come-out, she would be entitled to politeness, respect, and gratitude from Miss Amberly.

Claire had looked so pretty running up onto the lawn with her wild hair blowing behind her and the damp muslin clinging to her legs. He had felt like sweeping her up into the saddle and kissing her as roughly as she deserved. But no matter. She would marry soon enough and be no end of trouble to her husband. Then George could pursue his own concerns in peace.

Lady Diana sat at the table in the spare but cheerful breakfast room of de Vere House looking through the piles of visiting cards and invitations that had accumulated on her silver tray during the few days she had been at her mother's. Calmly she sorted them into piles of those requiring no action and those requiring replies. On the table in a cup ringed with purple violets, her second cup of tea grew cold. Across the room Darcy Desmarais sat cutting up a slice of ham.

Diana took the pile of those communications requiring replies and reviewed each one, dividing them again. Colin Quartermayne sauntered in. He was wearing immaculate morning clothes, and he began to regard himself in the mirror over the mantel with something very like distaste.

It was not surprising that Lady Diana was popular. Her fortune would have made her welcome even if she had been old and ugly; it was one of the greatest in England—left her by her young husband, Charles de Vere, who had gone down with his ship on a mission off the coast of Portugal. People who supposed that Lady de Vere had not wished to remarry in order to be independent were surprised when she remained in mourning for a year and a half longer than custom required. The truth was that Diana still hoped that Charles lived and would return to England.

Quartermayne turned and regarded himself from the other side.

"What is the matter this time? Looks *comme il faut* to me," observed Desmarais.

"The damnable lapels are too narrow. I shall have to send it back."

"Weston won't like that above half," said Desmarais.

"Just *comme il faut* is not good enough for me, and

55

he should know it," grumbled Quartermayne. Desmarais got up to leave the room.

"Before you go," interrupted his sister, "which of these would you prefer to accept for next week? I suppose it should be Lord Salisbury's affair or this one—for a houseparty at Oakhaven."

"Oh, not Salisbury," said Quartermayne. "He is a dead bore."

"So Howard's still dangling after your fortune," said Desmarais.

"Oh, do be quiet, Darcy. I've known George Howard since he was in short coats, and besides, he means to offer for Patricia Leland."

"According to Lady Patricia, at any rate. For a close-mouthed girl, she has told half the ton," Desmarais replied, "but I still think Howard is cherishing a *tendre* for you. Why else were we invited?"

Quartermayne scowled. "I went riding with Lady Patricia yesterday. She is also invited, and I hear that Ross has suddenly acquired a ward of marriageable age—one, if I quote the description correctly, 'prettier than most of this year's debutantes.'" Desmarais groaned. Thinks we were invited because of him, thought Quartermayne. Since it did not appear to him that Howard and Desmarais were friends, it must have been he, Lord Allenvale, whose company was the real object of Howard's invitation.

"I would like to go down," said Lady de Vere. "He plans to join a fox hunt, and Oakhaven is glorious country. We must bring our own hunters, however, because he says he hasn't enough."

"Ah, poverty," sniped Desmarais.

"What do you think of it?" Ignoring the gibe, Lady de Vere indulged in a rare smile of anticipation.

"If Lady Patricia is to be of the party, I should certainly accept," said Quartermayne.

"Well, I suppose we might," muttered Desmarais and stalked out of the room, nettled at being dragooned into a situation where he would be the guest of a man he had shot at, and a prey to husband hunters at the same time. It was a cursed presumption on Quartermayne's part to accept, he thought, as Howard had surely only included him in the invitation as a courtesy to Diana. Still, it was worth going to Oakhaven if it would make Diana happy. She had always been fond of Howard. Diana was born to happiness and bright hues. It pained her brother to see that she still wept easily and still wore gray. One thing was certain, and that was that Desmarais had begun to see Quartermayne for the encroaching mushroom he was. For all Quartermayne's taste and success with the ladies, Desmarais resolved that on their return from Oakhaven their guest would be staying elsewhere.

Chapter 10

Even though Claire feared the scorn of Lord Ross's guests, she had every intention of keeping her word to be civil to them. She had hesitated long enough over her fears. What if they did know of the Hartley matter? What if they did give her the cut direct? She had promised to face them and she must do it. Just the same Claire stood paralyzed on the tower stairs until Bettina shook her out of her reverie.

Downstairs Lady Patricia noticed that Lord Ross was not really listening to her news about London. He was waiting for something.

"I see you are not attending," she told him tartly. "I did not know I had become a dead bore."

By the time Miss Amberly made her entrance almost all the guests had arrived. When Lord Ross's ward appeared on the stair, Lady Patricia Leland was forced to admit to herself that Bettina's description had not done Claire justice. In her simple muslin dress, completely innocent of jewels, she stood poised as if to flee, and Lord Ross looked up with such sudden directness that Lady Patricia knew his ward was the cause of his abstraction.

Claire looked down and saw his blue eyes snap with annoyance. She could not know that his irritation was only because her lateness had made the thing she most dreaded, a grand entrance, a necessity.

Lady Patricia smiled with amusement at her *étourderie* as George introduced her to everyone. She thought cheerfully that if the chit had had as much countenance as beauty it would take less than a year to marry her off.

Claire was trying hard to show no sign of emotion. She knew she must not give George's guests the smallest sign that might lead them to believe she cared for him. To hold her composure was particularly hard because George had taken her hand in his as he led her about the room. It seemed to Claire as if her whole being was flowing toward him through her fingertips with an electric force that he must surely feel. But if Lord Ross felt anything, it did not show. When the introductions were completed, Claire found to her horror that she could not recall one single name. She was certain that her absentmindedness would swiftly be found out and construed as rudeness by Lord Ross.

Claire Amberly could not have been more dazzled if there had been a hundred guests instead of a mere fourteen. She had never seen such impressive people, and in the interval of light conversation that followed she tried to fit them to the names on the guest list. Dr. Westgate and Lord Ross she knew already, and Collins had described Lady Patricia Leland well enough, even if George had not distinguished her by his attention. She seems bored, Claire observed to herself—but even so she seems to radiate a kind of energy. It isn't just her lovely face that makes me want to look at her. She has a kind of concentration as well, like sunlight on a drop of water, bright and perfect.

Lord Edward Ashton was to take Miss Amberly in to dinner. As Claire had been told that on no account must she bore her dinner partner by mousy silence, she decided to enlist his aid. It was not Edward Ashton's habit to play at social oracle, but chance could not have given Claire a better teacher. From across the table, Lady Patricia saw her deep in conversation with Ashton, who looked thoroughly amused. Before long they were talking easily on other subjects. Claire was careful not to look too often in George's direction. He was sitting with Lady Diana de Vere, who was as beautiful a brunette as Lady Patricia was a blonde. It seemed to Claire that there had been stiffness between her guardian and Lady Patricia, but with Lady Diana he was as completely at ease as if she had been his sister. At that distance Claire could not hear what they were saying. On her right, Gerald Leland was talking about snuff boxes with Westgate, who collected them. Claire remembered that Gerald was heir to the Leland earldom and his sister's chaperon. His bland wife, Marianne, was seated next to a young gentleman Claire still could not place.

"Who is the man with the hilarious cravat, my lord?" she asked.

Lord Ashton laughed. "That is Colin Quartermayne, Viscount Allenvale, but if I were you I should not tell him what I thought of his clothes."

"Why not? What do you think he would do?" asked Claire.

"I shudder to think," grinned Ashton, looking forward to the occasion should it occur.

Claire was looking forward to making the acquaintance of the Buffington sisters, who were the only other young girls present. They had tiny, turned-up noses and beautiful satin slippers, and regarded her from down at the end of the table with wide-open, guarded eyes. Perhaps, if they liked her, she might learn how this society business was done. Beside Pamela, Viscount Desmarais looked marvelously at ease. In his brown velvet coat, he looked quite at home in the country salon, whereas Lady Buffington and most of the others, for that matter, looked clearly out of place, for all their fineness. Desmarais was treating Pamela to his crooked smile, and Claire could see that Lady Buffington was paying more attention to her daughter than to her dinner partner.

When the ladies went into the drawing room at the end of the meal, Claire shyly approached the Buffington sisters and began to ask them if they would like to ride around the estate with her in the morning. Before they had a chance to answer, their mother interrupted with a question about a governess they had once had and swept them to the other side of the room. Claire stayed where she was. She did not care to enter into any conversation about governesses. Instead, she attempted to engage Mrs. Leland in an attempt to find out something about George's intended which might be of use, but was only able to discover that Patricia rode well, and Marianne did not.

Claire was glad when the gentlemen rejoined the

party. Lady Buffington took this occasion to announce her plan—that each of the ladies should sing, or play. There was no harp, which would put dear Pamela at a disadvantage, but they would have to make do. Gerald favored this proposal with a rare smile. Desmarais, however, looked at the ceiling. He knew perfectly well that he and Quartermayne and Howard were the objects of this exercise, and it was a side of his elegibility he could do very well without. Quartermayne was better disposed to enjoy the performance. He smiled, and made eyes at Lady de Vere, who looked modestly away.

What George thought of the business Claire could not tell. He was standing toward the back of the room, next to Lady Patricia, and seemed content to let his guests arrange matters as they wished. The first lady to be prevailed upon was Lady Diana de Vere, whose soft, high-pitched voice was very pleasant. Lady Buffington sang—a bit too loudly. Marianne Leland performed a simple duet with her husband, which was much applauded for his artistry and her sentiment, and Alice Buffington played a long, complex piece on the pianoforte. Then Lady Patricia gave a fine rendition of a popular song. Her voice was very clear and fine, and Claire thought it would be difficult for Pamela Buffington to better the performance. Nevertheless, Pamela did. Her song, "Barbara Allen," was one all English people know, and she put such feeling into her voice that everyone except perhaps Westgate, who was tone deaf, was affected. The only problem was that the song had too many verses, and the audience became a little fatigued. Finally, Lady Buffington insisted that Miss Amberly must also sing or play. She refused politely, but Marianne, thinking her merely shy or modest, urged her to perform. In horror Claire crossed the room to her guardian.

"Please, G . . . , my lord, tell them I cannot play the pianoforte."

The corners of George's mouth turned down in a sardonic grin. "That is quite true. Miss Amberly does not play the pianoforte." His eyes told her it did not matter to him whether she sang or not, and suddenly

61

she became determined that these ladies should not make her look incapable.

"All right," she said finally, "I shall sing a cappella." Whereupon Claire launched herself into an Italian song, which (if one could understand the words) was at once outrageous and witty. It was one of the ones she used to sing to herself in the woods, and although she began it fearfully, very soon the gaiety of the melody penetrated her mood and allowed her to finish with something like defiance. Her audience was happily surprised, and she hurried to hide from their applause.

"*C'est une petite sauvage,*" observed Lady Patricia to Quartermayne.

"I suppose she is," commented Lord Ross softly. "Wild . . . like a wildflower."

Struck by the favorable interpretation George had given her remark, which had not been intended as a compliment, and even more impressed by his particularly poetic turn of phrase, Patricia came to the conclusion that whether Lord Ross and his ward were avoiding each other or not, Bettina had been right in her opinion. George was fond of her.

Later that evening when Desmarais came into the card room with Alice and Pamela Buffington, they found Quartermayne staring at the chessboard in disbelief. This schoolroom miss with whom he had been trifling had maneuvered him into a perfectly impossible position, probably quite by accident. He frowned as he attempted to think of the move least likely to alert his fair opponent to the fact that she could have him mated in four moves. Desmarais looked down at the board for a long moment and then laughed. Quartermayne moved his knight, and Claire, refusing to be distracted, checked his king with her rook.

"I wish I could play chess," said Pamela, looking into Quartermayne's pale blue eyes. He could see that she did not even know that he was losing.

"I could teach you," offered Desmarais.

"You could teach her to lose, like you always do," said Quartermayne.

"Do not be peevish just because you are outmatched," retorted Desmarais.

"Damn." Quartermayne had lost his habitual nonchalance. "I concede. Damn it to hell." Alice put her hands over her ears.

"You must not mind," said Claire dryly, "chess is only a child's game." Quartermayne did not trust himself to answer.

However, Desmarais was never at a loss. He smiled amiably. "If chess is a game for children, what would be a game for adults?"

"I suppose, love," she answered, and then blushed suddenly and deeply. Desmarais could not suppress a burst of laughter. After all, the chit was right. Claire, feeling that she had blundered onto dangerous ground, retreated in utter confusion up the hall stair.

"Lady Patricia was right to call her '*une petite sauvage*,'" said Quartermayne.

"What does that mean?" asked Alice.

"It's French for 'little savage,' stupid," advised her sister. ". . . And she is one, too. Did not even say good night."

Lord Ashton had just come in from the billiard room, followed by his host, in time to witness Claire's flight. "Flushed your game, eh?" he said to Desmarais.

"Not my game," asserted Desmarais. "Miss Amberly just beat Quartermayne at chess."

"She was uppish about it, too," put in Alice. "Said he behaved like a child."

"Bloody bad luck," grumbled Quartermayne.

"Do not be put out about it," George said equably. "She always beats me." Thereupon Lord Ross took Viscount Allenvale off to the billiard room.

Miss Pamela Buffington sat down in his place and Desmarais patiently instructed her until his sister importuned him to make a fourth at whist. He had already begun to find Pamela quite tedious. Miss Alice, who was just returned from sighting down the hall in hopes that Lord Ross would reappear, approached her sister. "She is not quite the thing, is she?" whispered Alice.

"Certainly not," answered her sister. " 'I suppose, *love!*' Perfectly shameless. At least she had the grace to blush. I guess she is a bit out of her depth with Viscount Desmarais."

That was the conversation George overheard when he came back down the hall. He thought with irritation that his ward had already asserted her marvelous talent for creating gossip. To add to his discomfiture, Alice Buffington attached herself to him, and remained tenaciously at his side until her mother arrived to send both girls to bed. Lord Ross then joined the whist party, which had enjoyed very good play, with Dr. Westgate as the principal winner. Gerald had retired early, to be with Marianne, who had the headache, so afterward George was able to enjoy a long interlude alone with Lady Patricia in the billiard room. Patricia had not spoken to him about the wedding arrangements, or entered into further argument about where they should live, and had been so captivating that George had forgotten completely that he had meant to ask her advice about Claire. Lady Patricia was wearing a new and exquisite perfume. More than anything George wanted her to enjoy herself in his house. Now that some of his friends were here, he realized even more how much he loved his home, and how badly it needed the grace and style of a beautiful woman.

Lady Patricia allowed him to kiss her, and permitted him to be more intimate with her than he ever had been before, but she would not go upstairs with him. George was disappointed, but he respected her for her refusal. After she had retired, he hung up the billiard cues.

"Respectability does not agree with me," he muttered. "Lady Leland was right."

Desmarais was in the library, his auburn curls illuminated by the firelight, his velvet sleeve draped casually over the arm of a chair, reading poetry in the dim light.

"You would look quite the romantic if your boots were not off," teased George.

"Confound my boots," said Desmarais. "I like your ward."

"She has more countenance than I supposed," he answered. "Everyone says she has been flirting atrociously with you."

Desmarais ignored the remark. Everyone flirted atrociously with him. "*Nouvelles fleurs parmi l'herbe nouvelle,*" he quoted dreamily. "Can she hunt?"

"She rides like an amazon," said George, "but I've never hunted with her."

"We will see tomorrow if she can outclass Lady Patricia," mused Desmarais. "I rather doubt it, but I am glad I came down."

George poured brandies for himself and Desmarais and they sat together staring into the fire and talking about sporting affairs. The heat of the fire made George's leg feel good. At last he stood up on it sleepily and said good night.

"I say, old man, do you speak Italian?" asked Desmarais unexpectedly.

George gave Darcy a sharp look. He did not quite like the sound of "old man."

"No," he said shortly.

"Well, I think I ought to tell you that the song Miss Amberly sang was not at all the thing."

George was thoughtful. "She does not sing. She did not want to sing. . . ." His voice was grave.

"Best singer in the house," Desmarais interrupted. "Heard her yourself . . . sings like a street boy. She is lucky none of the ladies understands Italian."

"She is just arrogant enough to assume none of us would, either," said George.

"Is she a bluestocking?"

"I think not," answered George, and as he went up the stairs he grinned to think that Lady Buffington's strategy had backfired. The butt of her trick had succeeded hugely with the very person before whom she had been most particularly intended to fail.

Chapter 11

"What a fine stallion," commented Desmarais, as Virgil was led out.

"Looks skittish to me," said Lady Buffington. "Who is to ride him?"

Lord Ross looked down at Lady Patricia, who was standing close by his side. As usual, she was an excellent judge of horseflesh. Her china blue eyes were sparkling with admiration. "Is he yours, my lord?" she inquired.

"Yes, but I mean to ride Hector as usual."

"I should like him, then," she said with decision.

Claire, who had come forward to take the bridle from the stable boy, paused in consternation.

"Surely you had better not," Lady de Vere advised her friend. "He looks too spirited for a lady."

Lord Ross was a little taken aback. "I must confess that Virgil is Claire's usual mount. She used to exercise him for my brother. He is obedient enough with her, so I suppose it is better if Claire takes him this morning."

Claire Amberly mounted Virgil, a little downcast at first, to think that the one accomplishment she had regarded as acceptable was placing her once again outside the realm of ladies. Her lip trembled, ever so slightly, but she kept her chin high, staring off into the woods so that no one would notice. Lady Patricia did have good taste. Claire wondered if George's decision in her favor had been because he did not credit her with enough manners to accept being assigned to one of the hired hacks without demur; or because he feared for Lady Patricia's safety, if she were to have her way. She wished there were some way George could know, without her daring to tell him, that she would not complain at anything he decided.

The horses were eager to be off. Claire held Virgil in check for a decorous beginning, but soon she and Desmarais had outdistanced the others and were speeding effortlessly across the open part of Oakhaven Park. Lady Patricia gazed ahead at them. "I could have managed him," she commented mildly.

"I am sure you could, but unfortunately my ward would have been put out if she had not been permitted to ride her favorite," explained George.

Lady Patricia smiled politely at her escort, as they watched the riders ahead of them taking a low wall. Inwardly she simmered with resentment at the slight she had received. That a penniless, gauche child should be preferred to her should not have to be borne. The girl was obviously spoiled, and should have been sent to school to learn a more submissive attitude. It was a pity Miss Amberly was now too old for school.

The party could still see Desmarais and Claire, who were now far ahead and had begun racing wildly.

Edward Ashton turned to George in amazement. "You sly dog," he grumbled. "That one could win the Davis point-to-point! Where have you been hiding him? And by the way, your ward can really ride! Lady de Vere and Lady Patricia are good, but I'll warrant Miss Amberly could be in at the kill!"

George answered quietly, "I do not think she has ever been at a fox hunt."

"I can scarcely believe it," said Marianne Leland.

"I'd better go 'round and pick up the pieces." George grinned and rode off in the direction he expected them to turn.

Desmarais boisterously jolted Virgil with his horse as they rode down the forest path. Breathlessly, he said, "You ride like a centaur. We should make love like centaurs."

Claire was fairly sure that Desmarais was joking. She had no fear of him, as she had written him off as a trifler. Still she was thrilled by her exercise.

67

"With centaurs—is it not just the horse part that makes love?" she retorted.

Desmarais laughed. "Then the human part must be innocent," he said, reaching for her to kiss her. Startled, Claire brought her whip down across his horse's nose. It sheered off, wheeling and bucking so outrageously that it was all Desmarais could do to keep his seat. Claire's laugh stopped abruptly as she looked up and saw George approaching through the trees. She did not know how much he could have seen or heard. Desmarais let discretion and his horse carry him some distance off.

"Luring people to their deaths again, Claire?" asked George lightly.

"I . . ." she began.

"Never mind, I saw what happened. You have been behaving like a shameless tease. Do you want to be seduced?"

"If you think I would let your friends seduce me because they are viscounts, I can tell you I would not!" she said rudely, furious that he should have felt the need to interfere.

George was stung. The girl had no worry for her virtue, apparently. It did not occur to her that she might get into a situation she could not control. . . . He lowered his voice. "By the way, he understands Italian. You ought to get to know people better before you show contempt for them by singing a song like the one you chose last night. I know you dislike being told what to do, but you did promise to be civil."

Claire's cheeks flamed. George had struck home. No wonder Desmarais had looked for a wanton in her. The shame she had tried to disguise with anger came flooding up, and George could see that he had succeeded all too well in his reprimand. He did not want his ward to burst into tears.

"Go back to Oakhaven," he said sternly, "but first promise me you will not ride unchaperoned again while my friends are here." She turned to go, but swiftly he caught her arm. "Give me your word," he demanded, "and do not dare to strike Hector across the nose!"

"Let me go, George; I will do as you say." The

words came out in a rush of fear, and when he released her she urged Virgil swiftly in the direction home.

With a feeling of deep dissatisfaction, George turned back to join his guests, and as he did so, he saw that Lady Patricia had come up behind him. She realized he must be wondering what she had heard. Patricia was surprised that he did not mention the incident, and supposed with annoyance that he did not wish to share his feelings with her. Well, the chit certainly was tiresome, and best forgotten. Nevertheless, on the way back Lady Patricia could not resist twitting Desmarais about the welt on his horse's nose, but she was careful to do it as if she had no idea what had taken place.

Later that morning Lord Ross and Lady Patricia went on an excursion in the neighborhood, chaperoned by her brother Gerald and his wife, in another phaeton. George took obvious pleasure in showing Patricia his favorite places. His attention was as much on them, many of which he had not seen for years, as it was on her, and she was reminded that she was resolved to reside only in London. Instead of evading the chaperones for another pleasant interlude, she found herself immersed in a heated discussion with George on the subject of architecture. He told Patricia in no uncertain terms what he thought of Morson House and all those other flimsy stucco imitations of Italian villas. "This is not Italy," he told her, and did not see why she should be miffed because they did not agree. As a result, Patricia was surprisingly standoffish with him. Indeed, she found she could even look forward to that half-penny ball he was planning in that barn he called Oakhaven, since it would afford her the occasion of testing his affection. It would be amusing to see if he could still be made jealous.

Claire Amberly was not upset by the reprimands she received from George Howard. She was used to being treated as a child, accustomed to being corrected, and she could tell from his eyes that George did not bear her any ill will because of her error in riding off with Viscount Desmarais. She almost wished her guardian had used it as a pretext for forbidding her the ball, the prospect of which filled her with terror. Claire sat for a long time, submitting to Bettina's ministrations. The maid was determined that her mistress should appear with a fashionable hairstyle. As she combed, curled, and pinned, Bettina chatted amiably with Claire, giving her opinions on all the young men. "Viscount Desmarais is very handsome, and he rides very well, but I think his face is too thin, don't you?" she mused. Claire agreed. "Lord Ashton is too fat, and he's married, you know," continued Bettina.

"Did I tell you he has invited the whole party to his estate for a ball that will take place on Friday?" asked Claire.

"No, miss. Will Viscount Allenvale be of the party? He is a regular out and outer for my money," said Bettina.

"He must have to spend hours on his hair, like me," said Claire bitterly.

"Don't you like Lord Allenvale?" persisted the maid.

"I suppose I ought to but I do not," Claire stated.

"If Lord Ross spent as much time on his appearance, I think he could be handsome," went on Bettina. "Except for that scar of his. If it were smaller, he might be able to hide it. I hear Alice Buffington has been following him around, and that Lady de Vere has been in love with him for years, but I don't see why. He's careless about his appearance. Do you like Lord Ross, Miss Claire?"

"No," Claire answered dully. "Like" was not exactly the word for the way she felt.

Bettina repeated this conversation to Lady Patricia while her mistress was downstairs, and was rewarded with a shilling. Claire had gone to present herself to George, and since he had also finished dressing early, she was lucky enough to find him alone.

"Am I passable, George?" she asked him.

George raised one eyebrow. "Your hair is not right," he said.

"But Bettina says this is the way I should wear it with this dress," objected Claire.

70

"It is too elaborate. Do you like it yourself?" he asked. Reluctantly, Claire shook her head. "It is your hair, not hers, Claire," he said seriously. "You will get nowhere in society if you allow servants to order you about. Go straight up and require her to do it over."

Claire bit her lip and turned on her heel. She considered not coming down at all, but she knew that George would never permit that. Her guardian was right, as usual, but it was hard to tell Bettina that her work was unappreciated. It was harder to sit still to have it rearranged while the coaches were arriving below.

Lady Patricia Leland stood beside Lord Ross for a few moments as he welcomed his guests. As he introduced them—the flower of county society—to his lovely lady, in her rose-colored silk frock trimmed with myriad knots of ribbons, he noticed once more the fineness of her manners. Perhaps it was wrong of him to want to remove her from London. She was wasted where people could not understand the elegance of her taste. In a free moment Patricia chose to observe that Miss Amberly had said she did not like him.

"Did she say so to you?" he asked, with an edge of anger in his tone.

"No, to her maid. I happened to hear of it."

"It is not surprising," said George, more equably. "I disliked my guardian also." To Lady Patricia's disappointment, her remark failed to provoke him to give her his version of the morning's events. Lady Patricia comforted herself with the idea that if he were to think himself disliked, he might resent it.

At the ball, Lady Patricia was particularly charming to all Lord Ross' local guests. She danced twice with young Squire Reynolds and three times with Viscount Allenvale, but Lord Ross could see that she was stealing glances at him all the time, and guessed that her interest in them was simply to make him jealous. As a result he felt no anger, only a mild sardonic amusement. When he danced with her, distant as she was, he felt the pleasure of anticipation.

71

The rest of the time he spent playing host, resolutely avoiding Alice Buffington, and keeping a weather eye out for Claire, whose first ball this was, although no one mentioned it. He observed with satisfaction that she seemed to be losing her fear, but when he danced with her the once that etiquette demanded, she did not speak to him, as she was concentrating so carefully on the steps.

As the ball drew to a close, and her insouciance had provoked no sign of jealousy from George Howard, Lady Patricia became surer than ever that this was because his interest had been given elsewhere. No matter that he had not spoken to Claire all evening. He had made her change her hair—interfered, in fact, in her life so that she could appear to better advantage, and he had been angry at the thought that she disliked him. Lady Patricia observed bitterly that what she had thought was single-minded devotion to her on George Howard's part might not even last until their wedding. She resolved that she would not stand idly by allowing him to make a cake of himself with his own ward.

Chapter 12

On the day after the ball it rained rather hard. The house was still full of the chrysanthemums that had been brought in to decorate for the ball—so many that Colin Quartermayne said they made the house smell bad. He retreated into the library to read, where he was discovered by Lady Patricia, who gazed about the room bored with cards, billiards, music, and everything else on Lord Ross's godforsaken estate. George had really managed the little ball excessively well without female assistance. He had done better with music and food than she had believed possible outside London, but George's talents as a host were wasted on such dull company. It was too bad that he had been distracted to the point where flirting atrocious enough to make her brother Gerald remark on it had failed to elicit the slightest mark of notice from George.

Out of the salon floated the stilted strains of Alice's effort on the pianoforte. She was, Lady Patricia surmised, attempting the overture to *The Marriage of Figaro*.

"What is so interesting about that book?" asked Lady Patricia.

Quartermayne understood that he was commanded to offer her attention, and instantly got to his feet. He kissed her hand in greeting. Lady Patricia smiled. George almost never kissed her hand, and she liked it. "It is a forbidden book actually," he confided. "I think you would like it."

"I? A forbidden book?"

"It concerns a man and a woman who attempt to seduce virtuous people. They consider it a challenge. Of course they are exposed in the end but the point is the strategies they use. That is why I think it will amuse you. You are full of stategies." He placed the volume in her hand. Colin Quartermayne had a way of presuming too much on their friendship, which had only just begun, but Patricia was somewhat flattered by his description of herself as a strategist.

"Perhaps it would be diverting. . . ." she said, allowing him for a moment to put his arm around her and draw her close to him.

That evening after supper, when the ladies entered the drawing room, Lady Buffington seated herself closest to the fire, on its left-hand side. There, flanked by her daughters, she planned to hold court. Opposite her, Lady Patricia and her sister-in-law took up their places as if by prearrangement. Next to Lady Patricia, who looked particularly delicate in her apple-green gown, her friend Lady de Vere was engaged in embroidering white rosebuds on a christening dress for the child of her cousin, Lady Devereux.

"Have you seen Lady Devereux recently?" inquired Lady Buffington, casting about as usual for choice bits of gossip. It was the latest *on dit* that Devereux had stepped into Lord Ross's place as Lady Montgomery's favorite.

"Yes, I have," said Lady de Vere.

"My, that is beautiful lace," commented Pamela.

"And how does she go on?" insisted Lady Buffington.

Lady de Vere raised her eyes from her work. "Blue-deviled, when I saw her last," she replied, since she saw no help for it.

"Let me see," went on Lady Buffington inexorably, "there was Lady Hoxham, and then that cyprian— What was her name? and now lady M——"

"I suppose it is an ill wind that blows no one good," cut in Lady Patricia. Marianne laughed.

Alice Buffington said angrily, "Lord Devereux is the most awful rake! He surely deserves to go to hell!"

Diana had left off working and was staring into the fire, her face gentle and sad. Claire remembered that

74

she had heard that Charles de Vere had died in Portugal and wondered if Diana were thinking of him. "I wonder what hell reserves for rakes," mused Diana de Vere.

"Dr. Westgate informs me that you have read the *Divina Commedia*, Miss Amberly. Perhaps you could enlighten us," commanded Lady Buffington.

"Surely it must be the worst place," whispered Pamela.

"In Dante's hell the lowest place is for traitors— Judas and Brutus are there, but . . ." Claire paused to think for a second. ". . . Perhaps the lowest place is not really the worst. I fancy Dante was more interested in making the punishment fit the crime. Rakes . . ."

At that moment the door opened and the gentlemen entered the room. Colin Quartermayne said, "Do go on, Miss Amberly. I am all agog to hear what you have to say about rakes."

"Blister me if I can figure out how she would know anything about us," said Desmarais, smiling. Alice Buffington looked shocked. Lord Ross laughed. Claire found herself unable to say a word.

Alice said, "We were discussing what the punishment in hell might be for a rake."

"Is there one?" said Quartermayne.

"Perhaps—to fall in love with a harlot," said Lord Ross.

"Of course," laughed Edward Ashton.

"You men are awfully silly! There would not be any harlots in hell," stammered Alice.

"Why else do you think so many men go there?" quipped Patricia with an angelic smile.

"Really, this conversation is most improper," asserted Lady Buffington, forgetting that it was her own taste for impropriety that had started them off on the subject.

Lady de Vere retired to her room soon after that with a severe headache. She had known these headaches to last for days, and was particularly annoyed at the possibility that this one might force her to miss the hunt, the major reason she had come to Oakhaven in the first place. Stretched out, with her

75

eyes closed, she could hear shouts and laughter from the salon, where the company was playing charades.

When the charades game was over and Lady Patricia was certain that Claire had retired, she sent Bettina to the tower room with Quartermayne's novel, a sheet of notepaper inserted under the cover, with these words written on it in lonely splendor: "Is it a sin to love?" and under this a cursive initial which was ambiguity itself. She thought with amusement of what would happen if Miss Amberly were to realize the book's immoral quality and attempt to return it without Lord Ross's discovering that she had seen it. Miss Leland went to bed laughing.

Claire was unable to guess the origin of the book, although she was certainly curious. She suspected that Bettina knew and had promised not to tell, but it was no matter. Actually she thought it more probable that it had been delivered to her by mistake, but she had had so little of interest to read lately that she decided to sample it. She found the style literate and the events interesting. If the moral tone were different from any book she had read before, this bothered her not at all.

Chapter 13

Early in the morning of the fox hunt, George went down to the stable to see that his arrangements were being adhered to. In the doorway to the main building Claire was shyly waiting for him. He realized that since his house party began, he had spent no more than two minutes alone with her. Well, it could not be helped.

"George, may I stay behind today, please," she whispered. George gazed at her curiously. Claire had not used his Christian name in front of the others, except for once—almost—when she had been asked to sing, and he had suspected that she had stopped doing it because she was vexed with him. The girl was meeting his curious glance, her dark eyes trusting, only her lips a little wary of the smile that seemed to be forming there. She was carefully dressed in her riding habit and ready to do as he decided.

"If you go with us, Ashton will show you how it is done. I do not think you would have any trouble."

"I am a little tired. Perhaps Lady Patricia could have her wish to ride Virgil. . . ." The suspicion of a smile had gone from Claire's mouth. George could tell she did not approve of the idea she was advancing. He decided it might be well to encourage the child in her moment of generosity. Perhaps it might bring Patricia closer to Claire if the girl did her a favor.

"All right. Do not go, if you do not wish to," he told her curtly, and hurried past her on his way. He had hoped that the hunt would show Claire to advantage, but it was equally possible that it could have been the occasion for another gaffe on her part.

Immediately Claire returned to her room, where she put on old clothes, tied a scarf around her curls like a peasant, and set off for the ruined church. Before the hunting party left Oakhaven for its rendezvous, Claire was lost from view among the trees.

The day was gloriously warm. Soft cream-puff clouds scudded along low above the hills, and the hunting party made an enthusiastic start, with Edward Ashton and Gerald Leland, resplendent in their red coats, taking the lead. Lady Patricia was the only lady from the Oakhaven party who had chosen to accompany them, so George was more aware of her than ever. Mounted on Virgil, she seemed more vivid, more alive, than she ever had when they were riding together in the London parks. The hunter was a little edgy under his unaccustomed rider, but she was holding him with a firm hand, and her face, suffused with effort and a kind of suppressed delight made George wish they were not going fox hunting. Still, it usually took an exciting event like a fox hunt to create that sort of joy on Lady Patricia's face.

Patricia's pleasure was not entirely in contemplating the excitement of the hunt. Since Lady Diana had remained indisposed, Patricia was supremely aware of being the only lady of quality in the party, as Lady Reynolds surely did not count. It did not bother her to be the center of the curious eyes of such worthies as Sir Henry Hartley and his loutish son Robbie. No, she gloried in it. Besides, she had just had a rather amusing idea. Suppose she encouraged this wild jumper to run away with her, just a little? Lord Ross would certainly follow her rather than the hunt, and so would Lord Allenvale. It would be interesting, she thought, to find out which of them showed the greater eagerness to "save" her. In fact, Patricia, despite her erect carriage and invincible air of superiority, was finding Virgil a little difficult to control, and much more tiring to ride than she had anticipated. George noticed her effort and respected her courage, if not her judgment, in choosing a mount a bit beyond her. He resolved to keep an eye on her in case the stallion proved troublesome.

The hounds were on the scent of the fox, which led them on a hard ride through fields and gardens, over and through gates, and just as the hunt seemed to be gaining on the fox, the wily beast cut up a creek to the north. The hunt turned to follow, but Virgil kept right on down into the valley and up the low hill opposite it. Patricia did not call out, but it appeared to George that Virgil was running away with her. In truth she had to exert all her considerable ability to stay on the sidesaddle. George turned his horse to follow, but he was the only one to do so. Virgil leaped the brook, as was his custom, and Patricia fought for control. She decided she did not wish to be run away with after all. However, it was too late. She was jolted horribly, her bonnet ripped askew by a stray branch, and holding on in fear for her very life, she continued willy-nilly up the hill where Virgil, in hellbent exuberance seemed determined to take her. Just short of the summit, Hector caught them up, and George stopped Virgil with practiced ease. Lady Patricia dismounted, and he swept her into his arms.

Unfortunately Lady Patricia's sense of romance had been spoiled. She was far too shaken up, and her hat was hanging by one pin! "What a fright I must look," she grumbled, attempting to restore it. George kissed her heartily by way of answer. He let her see to her coiffure, and then took her in his arms in earnest. George was fairly sure that the episode was intentional, but it made him happy to feel that she had wanted him to follow her; she wanted his attention that much. This is what she hoped would happen, he thought with amusement, and she doesn't like it above half.

The couple found themselves on a hill near the ruined wall of an old boxlike church. Part of the bell tower remained standing, but most of the nave was little better than rubble, overgrown with ivy.

Unexpectedly George looked up and saw Claire, on her knees in her dirty apron, her eyes as wide and dark as stormy waves at sea. When she saw that he had noticed her, she got to her feet, ready to flee.

Lady Patricia turned and said, "Well, child, were you saying your prayers?"

"Perhaps I should have been," she answered.

"What brings you to this lovely spot?" inquired Patricia.

Claire flushed. George was surprised that his ward was not provoked into rudeness. Instead she said shyly, "I guess you could see it. It is laid out inside the nave." Lady Patricia was a little taken aback. She and George entered the ruined church, where they stared down at the gothic window, which reflected the morning sun.

"That is remarkable," said Lady Patricia, "but what do you do it for?"

"I like it better than anything I could make with a needle," said Claire. Standing together, both blonde, hatless, and wild-haired, with their skirts spattered with mud, they could have been taken for sisters. George was charmed by the sight of them.

"George, please do not tell the vicar. He would never understand."

George smiled. "No, of course not."

"You should not call your guardian 'George.' It is improper," said Patricia sharply, "and Virgil has behaved very ill."

"He has always been used to coming here. I must apologize for not teaching him to behave better," replied Claire, with a tilt of her chin that belied the humility of her words.

"What you do not know, you cannot teach!" returned Lady Patricia. As the two females under his protection faced each other like bantam cocks, George gazed down at the king's image, which glittered in true colors under the autumn sun.

"I like him," said George with conviction.

"You should, my lord. He has been broken in more places than you," said Patricia lightly. Neither girl could see the expression on George's face, which was still turned down over his find, and when he stood up the pain was gone, and in its place was a slight sneer—Claire thought—for her broken and misguided efforts.

Patricia remounted the unruly Virgil in a fit of brave determination. She rode away slowly and imperiously, her back straight. George's eyes lingered for a moment on the figure of the king.

"Do not worry about it; she is not herself," he said without smiling.

Claire turned her face away from him. "On the contrary, I find her very much herself," she said evenly.

George mounted Hector and rode after Patricia. For a long time Claire stared after them and watched the long grass blow where they had ridden away.

Chapter 14

The next morning, another spectacularly beautiful one, almost the entire party went out for a morning ride. It was a large party and a narrow trail, so it was natural that there should be some straggling; the younger, more enthusiastic riders steadily diverging from the older group, which included Lady Buffington, Dr. Westgate, and out of politeness, their host. A bold chill wind was blowing out of the bright sky, with gusts that tore leaves from their twigs and made them fall all around the riders like flakes of snow. Desmarais's blue coat clashed with the blue of the sky, and Marianne's dark red habit seemed to call out to the leaves of sumac and ivy, Claire thought. Quartermayne's wine-colored suit reminded her of the smell of the wild grapes that grew on the way to the ruined church. Musing about the appearance of the younger members of the party, Claire held back to view them from a distance. She decided that stained glass could not have caught it. One would have to have paint. Then she speeded Virgil a trifle to catch them. Much as it irked her, she had promised George not to ride unchaperoned.

Desmarais and Quartermayne raced ahead across a field, while Gerald and the ladies slowed their pace, talking. At this point the path was scarcely wide enough for two, so Claire politely kept behind. After a short distance, Marianne turned back, feeling tired, and Gerald with her. Since Claire did not particularly care to be left in Patricia's company, she nearly decided to go with them. However, she could not pretend that she was tired. On a day like this she could ride for hours. What she hoped and expected was that

Lady Patricia would ride ahead to catch up to the men.

Lady Patricia looked ahead of her with annoyance, listening to Virgil's hoofs on the forest floor. Why is Claire following in this irritating manner? she asked herself. Glancing back at George's ward, whose ominously quiet demeanor and cold gray eyes gave no clue to her motives, Lady Patricia was reminded of their first ride, the byplay with Desmarais, and George's anger. George had told the chit not to ride alone, Patricia remembered. Of course.

Suddenly and maliciously Patricia spurred her mount, heading away at a pace that sent the ribbons of her dainty bonnet whipping out behind her. Claire followed. Virgil could easily keep up with the mare, but when Claire saw Lady Patricia's stubborn and cheerless efforts to outdistance her, she gave it up. After all, she could probably return to where Gerald and Marianne were in a few minutes. At a slight widening of the path she turned Virgil aside and checked his speed, turning back the way she had come. Bad manners as it was to ride alone, she thought it was worse to stick where she wasn't wanted.

The foliage was thick above her, and Claire rode through it as through a dark vault, glancing about her now and then to enjoy the colors in small dramatic patches of sunlight that now and then penetrated the roof of leaves. Unexpectedly she found herself staring into a frame of shivering beech leaves, which centered on Desmarais's curious, playful eyes. His horse, breathing easily, was nose to nose with her own. Claire realized he had waited for her.

"What frightened her?" he asked.

"She was not frightened, my lord, except perhaps by the prospect of continuing to be bored by my company." A stray curl blew into her eyes, and she brushed it aside.

"I doubt if you bore her. . . ." he answered.

"Do not let me stop you from following her," interrupted Claire. "I am going back anyway."

"In fact I doubt if you can bear her," Desmarais went on.

Claire laughed. "You are rude, my lord," she replied, "but I doubt if you are in earnest. Are you ever in earnest?"

"Hardly ever," returned Desmarais. At that moment George came riding up the path by himself and saw them staring into each other's eyes with obvious appreciation, while coppery leaves sailed all about them on the rising wind. Again Claire had ignored his warnings. Again she had stubbornly set his authority at naught. He would have to show her that she could not defy him so simply. Desmarais's eyes were wide with surprise at the anger on his host's face. Claire said nothing, but squared her shoulders and flashed a black glance of her own. Meeting George like this was the sheerest bad luck.

"Go and stable your horse," George said to Claire, in a low, falsely casual voice. "You will not be riding him for a while."

In spite of herself Claire flushed, and returned to Oakhaven without a word.

Desmarais began to whistle.

At afternoon tea, the company admired the bowl of small red roses that Claire had put on the table. "I saw them in the garden yesterday," observed Marianne.

"Why not leave them there, in all their delicate splendor?" asked Alice Buffington. Quartermayne groaned, casting a conspiratorial glance at Patricia, who was sitting with Desmarais on the far side of the room.

"Because I expect a hard frost tonight," answered Claire.

"But, I mean, why *cut* roses? They are so fabulously lovely in their natural setting."

"If you cut them, they keep blooming, but if you leave them alone, they die and go to seed," explained Claire. As she said this Lord Ross entered the room quietly. He had just come from the assizes, where he had been unable to prevent one of his laborer's sons

84

from being transported for poaching on the Reynolds land. He was in a foul humor but hoped it did not show.

"Is that so also of Rosses?" asked Diana, looking up at George with an affectionate smile.

"No," said George lightly, pouring himself some tea, "If you cut a Ross, it leaves a scar."

"I think the scar makes your face more . . . interesting," decided Alice Buffington. George smiled obliquely at Alice, who returned his expression with interest.

"Lord Ross would be gothic enough without a scar," quipped Patricia.

Diana laughed. Claire gazed down sadly at the bowl of roses, wishing she could change the subject.

The conversation ran lightly elsewhere, and thinking himself unobserved, George found himself sneaking looks at the downcast girl and regretting her sorrow. I am a bad guardian, he thought, but if I never chastized her, I would have no control over her at all. After finishing his tea, George got up and left the room to change, still frowning slightly.

Across the room in his quiet corner, Viscount Desmarais turned to Lady Patricia. "Are you sure you want to form an alliance with a thundercloud?"

Patricia looked up in surprise. Desmarais's question was impertinent; his tone was more so, but he had spoken quietly, so that the others could not hear, and seemed to be awaiting her answer with genuine interest. "I suppose the assizes were excessively unpleasant. I told him not to go," she commented tartly.

"It is not the assizes, it is his ward," continued Desmarais. "If he does not allow her to flirt, how does he expect to marry her off? Did you know he has forbidden her to ride?"

"For flirting with you?" asked Patricia rudely.

"I suppose so." Keeping his voice low, Desmarais went on to describe their nasty encounter in the woods that morning. "So you see," he concluded with an impish grin, "you have competition, my lady!" Unable to hide her consternation, Lady Patricia got up and stalked out of the door, her curls swinging, and drew every eye in the room.

"Damned if you are not the most complete hand, Darcy. Wish I could rattle her like that myself," drawled Quartermayne.

Desmarais chuckled. The trouble with Ross, he thought, is that he is so used to gambling that he could not show his hand if he wished to, and the trouble with you, my lady, is that you refuse to gamble at all. You want everything to be absolutely sure.

Chapter 15

Lady Patricia had thought all day on the subject of this silly penchant of George Howard's for Claire Amberly, which no one else seemed to be aware of. When Viscount Desmarais had told Patricia the particulars of their disagreeable little confrontation in the woods, an idea began to ferment in her mind. It was the outside of enough that George should be so obviously jealous of Claire and that puppy Desmarais and show no such feeling toward her—when she had given him the most obvious provocation!

It appeared that her intended had formed the idea that Claire was disobedient and defiant. The chit had seen George take Patricia in his arms and kiss her. No wonder Claire wanted to do the same thing. George believed his ward had deliberately broken her word not to ride unchaperoned. Perhaps if Claire were to go one step further in disobedience, it would be all over between them. Then there would no longer be any question of a London come-out for the little savage, who would never "take" in any case.

George could leave his ward in the country and forget her, and Claire's presence would give him an aversion to Oakhaven that would accustom him to stay in London. The girl would eventually run off with some local lout, which perhaps was just what she was fit for, but how could all this be achieved? Lady Patricia pleaded an indisposition and retired to her rooms to think. She would have to work very fast, as their party was to leave for Ashton Manor the following afternoon.

It was clear that the obvious way for Claire to defy George would be to ride her horse, since George had forbidden it. Bettina thought it would be impossible to induce Claire to do this, so there was nothing for it but a masquerade. Bettina could easily obtain Claire's habit and insure that she stayed in her room. Then Patricia could go out in Claire's place. It would be best, thought Patricia, if Claire were seen *tête-à-tête* with a man, and Dr. Westgate was the logical choice. The doctor had been seen conversing with her often enough in their mysterious Italian. In fact, Claire had shown more interest in the doctor than in any other guest save Desmarais. It was unfortunate that Viscount Desmarais was absolutely out of the question; he slept much too late. Patricia thought it was too bad she couldn't include that arrogant young idiot in her scheme as well.

Lady Patricia went down at once to talk to the doctor, pretending that her indisposition was the reason for the interview. He was surprised at her request to join him on his morning ride, but he knew her to be on the verge of marriage and guessed that perhaps Lady Patricia was having apprehensions about childbirth or some such thing. He knew perfectly well that she had no interest in him, and so had no qualms about agreeing not to mention the outing.

Next Patricia knocked on Diana's door. She explained to her old friend that she was going riding with the doctor, in order to persuade him that his attentions must cease, but because George was so very jealous, she wanted to be sure that her intended did not suspect that she had gone riding with anyone. "If Ross asks you, I rode with you. I just want to spare him the worry. He's been so foolish!" said Patricia gaily. Diana agreed reluctantly, in a fair certainty that she'd never be called upon to lie, anyway. She was convinced that Patricia's ideas of George's jealousy were highly exaggerated. If they hadn't been, her friend would have been in the suds long before this.

Last of all, Lady Patricia secured Bettina's cooperation, telling the girl she planned a harmless prank. When Claire slept, her maid brought her riding habit to Patricia's room.

Before she retired, Patricia sat down to forge a note to Westgate from Lady Stanwich, whose gout was notorious and whose round hand easy to copy. When it was finished, she lay in bed, her heart beating fast at her own audacity. She felt flushed and damp with apprehension at breaking the rules to which she had been so strictly reared. Even if she had the ill luck to be caught, no one would think anything of it because she had good reasons all thought out. She lay in bed thinking of questions she might be asked. Answers raced through her mind, were chosen and discarded until at last she slept, while below the window of her room, on the lawn, George walked restlessly in his waistcoat and shirt sleeves, letting the wind blow through his hair, and watching the variations of the clouds, as they flowed around the coasting moon.

When Bettina had expressed surprise that morning at Claire's failing to go out for her usual ride, Claire told her that Lord Ross had forbidden it, and Bettina had seemed most indignant.

"He is cruel to you, miss," sympathized the maid.

"His brother was worse," said Claire darkly, remembering all the times Lord Edward had had her locked up, and the abject apologies she had been forced to make to him. "But somehow I minded it less with him. . . ." Her voice trailed off and she did not trust it any further.

"Would you like it if I brought your breakfast up to your room?" offered Bettina.

Claire thought it an excellent idea. She nodded. Why should she make it more difficult for them to talk about her? She hated the whole smug, artificial bunch. Perhaps one or two of the more charitable ones, like Dr. Westgate, would believe her indisposed.

Claire sniffed, and picked up the mysterious French novel. By the time Bettina appeared with a tray she was deeply immersed in it. Lying across her bed on her stomach, toasting her bare toes before the grate, and nibbling a piece of cold bacon she held in one hand, Claire considered the characters. Valmont was a rogue, but a likable one. However, the two young people were perfect idiots. It was too bad that was often the way in novels.

Claire wondered if her lack of experience made her seem as stupid as that to George Howard's sophisticated guests. Claire never noticed Bettina when she entered with the sullied riding habit and hung it in its usual place.

Downstairs, Wilson handed Dr. Westgate a sealed message. He opened and read it. "Damnation," he commented. "Lady Stanwich's cursed gout again. I wish she had chosen some other physician to be at her beck and call."

When Lord Ross came out of the breakfast room, he found Lady Patricia poring over the book of Italian gardens he had bought for Claire. Apparently deep in study, she looked up at his approach.

"My lord," she said, "there are so many interesting ideas in this book. I think we should have a summerhouse like this one, perhaps down by the pond." Lady Patricia looked very pretty. Her guinea-gold curls bobbed with unusual enthusiasm. Her cheeks were faintly flushed, bringing out the delicate pink of her morning frock. George smiled. Just as he had hoped, Lady Patricia was planning improvements for Oakhaven, but it was typical of her to fix on a purely decorative structure. George placed his hand over Patricia's, where it rested on the page. She pulled her hand from under his and looked up into his eyes. "I wonder what Miss Amberly would say to it?" she mused. "She knows the grounds here so well."

"I will call her and we shall find out," replied George.

"Oh, do not disturb the child on my account," said Lady Patricia politely.

George remembered that he had forbidden Claire her usual ride. "Never mind," he said, "she has nothing to do this morning." George called Wilson over to him, and sent for Bettina, who was told to ask Claire to come down at once. After about half an hour, Bettina descended reluctantly to inform his lordship that her mistress was nowhere to be found. Bettina's reluctance was not for lying, but for facing the anger in his face. She had incurred his displeasure once before, when she was caught listening outside the library door, but this time he wouldn't be angry at her.

When he heard that Bettina could not find Claire, George went at once to the stables, and inquired if Virgil had been taken out. Jim, who had been hired only the week before, told him that a blonde lady with a black habit had taken Virgil, but had returned from her exercise "a little bit ago," and had gone up to the house. Only one person at Oakhaven had a black riding habit. Only one blonde could handle Virgil—and that was George's ward.

"Was the lady alone?" he asked the stableboy.

"Wi' Doctor Westgate, my lord," he replied.

"The Devil!" George strode up to the house, leaving Jim gawking after him and wondering how he had offended.

At the house Wilson informed his master that the doctor had just left to attend Lady Stanwich's gout. In any case George did not really suppose that Westgate would have behaved dishonorably toward his ward, and could think of no other explanation than that Claire had simply wished to defy him. If she had told Westgate of his prohibition, the doctor would never have abetted her. Lady Diana was seated by the window working at her embroidery.

"Did you see Dr. Westgate on your ride this morning, my lady?" asked George.

"No, my lord," she answered, keeping her eyes on her work. How she hated the idea of lying to him. But perhaps it would not be necessary.

"Who did you ride with?" he persisted. She could see anger already on his handsome face, and pitied her friend Patricia. Charles De Vere had trusted his wife absolutely, before and after their marriage. "Patricia and I rode down by the river," she said flatly, hoping that would mollify him—but it seemed to have just the opposite effect. George turned on his heel and went up the stairs two at a time. He found Claire sprawled on the bed reading her book. George strode over to her side and jerked it out of her hand.

Nervously, Claire pulled her skirt down to cover the fugitive lace of her shift, and sat up in one graceful movement, her eyes wide with astonishment.

"Do not look so surprised. You know very well I sent for you. Why did you not come down?"

"I would beg your pardon, my lord, because I did not know you desired to see me," she said with spirit, "but you are so rude I do not think I should consider your wishes."

"Where did you go this morning?" he demanded, fixing her in the blue-hot flame of his furious eyes.

"I have been here all day," she retorted with a fury almost equal to his own.

George's anger increased. Just because she might have guessed that he was fond of her was no reason for her to flout him. He might be a bad guardian but he had tried. . . . "I dislike liars," he told her.

"How dare you call me a liar?"

"I told you not to ride, and you went out *tête-à-tête* with Westgate." His voice was rough with contempt.

Claire looked at George. She was at point non-plussed. How could he have gotten such an idea?

George fought back his anger. Quite an actress, he thought. She really does it very well. "I know all about it," he said cynically. It was disillusioning to think that someone whose innocence he had hoped to protect was in fact morally corrupt, disloyal, defiant, and a bare-faced stupid liar.

Claire went over to the wardrobe. "I can show you that I have not been riding," she said, pulling out the black habit. It had fresh mud on the hem. It seemed odd to George that Claire would behave so—so monstrously unreasonably—and he took it for mockery of a new and unheard-of kind.

"What is the matter with you, Claire?" he said harshly. "Why are you determined to make a fool of yourself?" As she forced herself to look across the room into his devastating eyes, Claire realized that only one person could have worn her habit in masquerade. It was cut too narrow in the waist for anyone but Lady Patricia.

"Oh, God," she said sharply, trying to match his

scorn. "*You* make a fool of yourself, listening to that deceitful Leland bitch!"

"*Not one more word!*" George shouted with a ferocity that left his ward breathless with fear. "Lady Patricia did not say a word to me about it. I am disgusted with you, Claire, and you will be punished. You will not ride Virgil again. He will go with me to Ashton's and you will remain here, as the demands on your abilities have been perhaps too great."

Lord Ross strode out and went to his own rooms, where he attempted to get himself in hand. At last when he began to see normally again, George realized that he was still holding Claire's book. It was one he had not seen in the house before, and he regarded it at first with curiosity and then with further shock. It was an English translation of *Les Liaisons Dangereuses,* a book so immoral that it could only be obtained from a sophisticate. No honorable woman would have given an innocent girl a forbidden book; Claire must have received it from a man. Convulsively, George threw the volume into the fire and watched it burn.

Chapter 16

Lord Ross did not see his ward for some time. Westgate and Lady de Vere had returned to their homes, and the party for Ashton's made ready to depart. Lady Patricia, leading the group, perched with Desmarais on the seat of George's phaeton, as the Buffingtons' coach and the servants' coach drew in behind it. Virgil was saddled outside, ready to leave, but for a moment George lingered in the hallway. He turned at the sound of footsteps above him on the landing. A pale face accosted him over the rail, and he squirmed inwardly at the thought of apologies. He resolved that no matter what excuse Claire tried with him, he would not change his mind. As he raised his eyes to see Claire's expression the slanting light made him squint. His eyebrows nearly met over his nose.

"My lord," she asked briefly, "was it Bettina you sent to look for me this morning?"

"Yes, Claire," he answered, fully expecting her to blame the maid. Instead she simply stared at him for a long moment and remounted the stair. He looked so fine in his Hessians and russet coat. It hurt her to turn away from him, but she had to do it. In any event, she could think of nothing to say that would have removed his frown.

From the tower window Claire watched George ride away between the oaks that lined the drive, and his image soon smeared across the browns and reds of their leaves in the blur of her tears.

When Bettina was dismissed, both Bennett and Randall were quite unable to account for it, and a bit put out that Miss Amberly had not told them why she had refused to give the girl a character.

"Let her get one from her other mistress," was all Claire would say, and insisted that Bettina leave Oakhaven that very evening.

Late that night, in front of her mirror, when all the servants were asleep, Claire stood snipping away at her hair, which fell in long locks to the floor. As she worked Claire remembered Lady Patricia in her jaunty bonnet calling out cheerfully to George, who was riding out ahead of the party, and heard in her mind Alice Buffington's voice—"Viscount Allenvale says they were together in the billiard room until *midnight!* Do you think I should *absolutely* despair of him, Pamela?"

Alice's sister had answered, "They are engaged, Alice, just as if it were in the *Gazette*, and it would have been announced before, except that Lord Leland is such a high stickler about mourning. You may not be as pretty as Lady Patricia but you are certainly just as accomplished, and much more agreeable. I think Lord Ross will be sorry after he is married that he did not offer for you."

"Then it will be too late!" Alice had moaned, and nothing Pamela said could console her.

Claire gathered up her hair cuttings and threw them into the grate, where they set up such a fearful stench that she was forced to open the window to air out the room. It does not smell any worse than I feel, she thought. Lady Patricia will be mistress of Oakhaven, and if this is a sample of her dealings, I had best leave while I can. George is a fool—but I can see why he would think I lied. I should not blame him for not believing me, but I do! He will ride to Ashton's and then spend the rest of the year in London. Without Virgil I will not be able to bear it!

But Claire knew that Virgil's absence was only a small part of her misery. She had tasted something strange and exciting—something that she had not known existed. All through the black and gray hours

95

of night Claire lay awake, and when dawn came she rose, wound a cloth tightly around her chest, and over it put on her homespun shirt. Then she put on the rough tweed breeches and the battered jacket and cap that she had acquired from a former stable boy. It was not the first time she had worn them; and now with her hair hacked off neatly all around she doubted that she would be taken for a female from a distance.

Before the servants were awake Claire Amberly started walking away from Oakhaven through the woods to the north, with the vague idea that she might find friends of her father's in Edinburgh, where she had visited once before her mother's death. But perhaps on the way she could find employment.

Claire's disappearance was discovered very promptly. It was not that anyone thought it odd that Miss Amberly should have left the house at such an early time. If it hadn't occurred to Randall's suspicious nature that Bettina had been dismissed for stealing some of her mistress's things she would not have attempted to take an inventory, and no one would have worried over Claire's absence. However, since Randall had kept the accounts when the new things were paid for, and had herself given many of the old ones to the parish, she knew just what Claire had, and her investigation showed that nothing at all was missing. The fact that Miss Amberly was out without any of her clothes was disturbing to say the least. Mrs. Randall remembered hearing Lady Patricia say that Miss Amberly would end in Bedlam, when her quarrel with Lord Ross was talked about. Randall sent Wilson and Hawkins to search the estate and the country around it, and when by ten o'clock they had been unsuccessful in finding the girl, Randall sent Hawkins to Ashton's to tell the master.

"'e'll not like it above 'alf," said Hawkins.

"I don't think you should go," said Bennett. "She'll come back 'ere by 'erself. She's angry with 'is lordship, but where else can she go?"

"No!" Randall insisted. "Lord Ross must be informed at once."

"Damn your eyes, Collins. I told you not to wake me. Get your motheaten carcase out of this room!" Collins took two steps back from the bed. His master had not retired until five the previous night, and the brandy he had drunk would of course be making him foul-mouthed and irascible. George groaned and rolled over on his belly.

"My lord," insisted Collins, "your ward . . ."

George sat up. "The devil fly away with my ward!" he spluttered.

Collins prudently took another step backward, and bowed respectfully to the disheveled and naked occupant of the elegant four-poster. "I beg your lordship's pardon for disturbing you so early, but Hawkins just rode down with an urgent message."

"All right, Collins," said George, holding his head. "What's the bloody message?"

"Miss Amberly has disappeared, my lord." Collins gave George the particulars, insofar as he had been told them. George groaned and began to drag himself out of bed. Very few people knew the provisions of Edward's will, but Simmons had made it crystal clear that Michael Howard was just waiting for a pretext to break it. The disappearance of a ward Lord Ross was bound to protect was just such a pretext—leaving out what Lord and Lady Leland would say to the business, if they should hear of it. George swore Collins to secrecy, left a brief note for Lady Patricia and dressed to depart.

It was a fabulous day. The grass on the downs was blowing in dry rustling waves, and thick gray clouds were chasing each other toward the east. The damp wind in George's face had just enough bite to wake him without chilling. His head ceased to ache, and after stopping at a posting house for breakfast, he felt a great deal better. He thought with irritation that by the time he arrived at Oakhaven, the servants would be sure to have found the girl. He sympathized with

Edward for perhaps the first time. Claire was playing games with him! He would teach her that this was neither wise nor profitable. He wondered if she would have behaved differently if she knew how much depended on his reputation at this time. George could remember times in his youth when he could cheerfully have done anything just so long as he thought it might inconvenience Edward. Certainly he would be a fool to give an angry and immature girl the information that it was in her power to ruin him.

Lady Patricia was the only one George had told of his reason for leaving Claire behind. He had wanted to be reassured that he had acted correctly. Patricia was so astute about people; it was nice to know she approved of his conduct.

"It is mad of her to defy you. I do not understand it," Patricia had said—yet his intended was not always sweet and understanding with him. She could often be demanding and caustic. George found himself wondering which was the real Patricia, the pure, proud, prudent and brilliant wit he had courted under such close supervision, or the wild woman he had glimpsed for the first time the previous night? George had never seen Lady Patricia so gay, so clever, so light of foot, so enamored—in fact, so wanton, and although George had for once been overshadowed by a woman, he had no resentment of it. It was simply that he had not perfectly liked what he had seen. Perhaps it was just that he had not really been in the mood to be gay. He had wanted to think. . . .

At Oakhaven, George learned that a thorough search of the neighborhood had turned up no trace of Claire. Randall took him aside and whispered about burned hair in the grate. "And my lord," she breathed portentously, "none of her clothes is gone! Now do you imagine I'd want to tell Hawkins that? Do you think the lass is mad?"

"No, Randall," he said impatiently. "You had best sit down and have a cup of tea. I will find her if she is to be found." With Hawkins' best hound, George set out through the wood. It reminded him of his years in the army. If only we could have been tracking something so beautiful then, he thought with a grin. The trail passed the ruined church, and then turned north. George rode on patiently, expecting the trail to stop at some house or inn in the vicinity, but it did not. He began to suspect that the beast had confused her scent with a rabbit's. If not, it was remarkable that his ward had had the energy to walk so far. George knew the neighborhood well. He wondered who she could have come here to meet, and pondered the unlikely possibility that Westgate should have a *pied à terre* in the vicinity.

George shrank from overtaking his ward. Reproaches and abuse would be inevitable, and he knew how much he hated female hysterics—he had provoked them in several of his former friends. In this case, he did not know how he should behave. It was different with lovers.

Chapter 17

Although she did not really expect to be recognized as a girl, Claire hesitated to approach any public places where food could be bought. Her only money was a five-pound note, and she feared people either might think it was stolen, or try to do her out of it themselves. Lord Edward had given it to her the last year at Christmas, and she had been a fool not to have changed it.

Claire was not worried about being followed by the servants, as they were accustomed to her long rambles out of doors. They would probably not even think about her until evening. It certainly did not occur to her that she might be followed by George Howard. She did not think she was important enough to him, even if he were aware of her departure.

Claire stopped to sit on a wall for a minute and kick the mud off her boots against the stones. Then she trudged on, over the furrows plowed for winter wheat, between cornstalks bent and bleached by the autumn wind, and through flaming oak woods, thinking that soon her path must intersect the north road, on which she hoped to beg a ride or walk to Edinburgh. She thought she remembered the man at the museum there who had been her father's friend. It was not much to go on.

Claire was becoming chilled and felt quite light-headed into the bargain, but it was no use thinking of going back to Oakhaven. She had already come much too far. So she pressed on, more slowly now, stopping often to rest, and looking about warily before crossing any country lanes. At about six o'clock she came to an abandoned orchard where apples still clung to the low black branches, and half-rotten ones glowed from the ground. Claire moved among them eagerly, selecting first one and then another in search of a good one.

That was how George saw her when he rode over the top of the hill—a small figure moving among the old gnarled trees in her shabby jacket. The dog barked his recognition, and Claire looked up to see a familiar horse and rider coming across the field. She thought her heart would stop. She had never dreamed he would care enough to come after her.

Claire fled headlong down the hill, through the orchard, over the fieldstone wall, and on into the rift behind it—a gravel quarry overrun with blackberry canes, which she pushed aside ruthlessly, not caring if she were scratched or not. After her came George, who from his higher vantage point could see a way to ride around the briars. Then Claire plunged heedlessly down the rock-strewn wall of the quarry, with stones slipping all around her. She moved with a sureness and confidence that amazed her guardian, who was forced to dismount at the quarry rim, where he told the hound to stay.

"Claire!" he called after her, and the sound of his voice echoed hollowly back over the distant clatter of her flight. George began to climb down the quarry wall, and reaching the base of it, began to run. Claire started up the other side recklessly, without testing her footing. It would be better to fall among the stones than face his scorn. At last she stumbled, and looking up, saw George quite close, running uphill after her in an awful limp, with his riding whip clenched in one hand.

Claire's face registered complete horror and she struggled desperately up. At last reaching a pine tree at the quarry rim she hauled herself up into its tarry and prickled interior.

George, who had been stopped by her horror-stricken glance, was now surer than ever of her complete aversion to him. He was furious with himself for having allowed her to see him limp. Now he had made himself completely repulsive. Claire was so young. *Her* body of course was perfect—but why it should have made such a difference to him George could not have said. In any case, his ward was caught. She would have to come down from her tree eventually. George continued up the quarry wall more sedately, and by the time he assumed a stance at the edge of the clearing under the tree, Claire could see that his wonderful composure was restored. It was just as if that grotesque limp had never been. Claire realized that although she had heard of his injury, she had never actually believed in it.

Claire had seen the anger on George's face, and knew she deserved it. She climbed higher into the tree, hoping to postpone the whipping she expected. Bitterness rose up in her again at the injustice of it all.

George needed all the authority he could muster to order the girl back to a situation they both knew was untenable. He was no fit guardian, but he would not be lied to and flouted. George felt more and more uneasy. The sun brushed the tops of the western hills, and the quarry began to look ominously dark. On its far rim the hound stopped barking.

"Come down out of that, or I will come up," growled George.

"Stay on the ground, little boy," she said with airy defiance, "or you will spoil your suit."

Suddenly the impact of George's body shook the tree. As he stormed up one side, Claire climbed and slid down the other. About ten feet above ground she lost her grip and fell sprawling on the thick pad of pine needles below. George was beside her in an instant. At first all Claire could do was fight for breath. At length she looked up. George was wearing an expression she dreaded as much as his frown, and she was too winded to move. He could do whatever he wanted with her.

"Wretched brat," he said gently. Claire was bleeding from a scratch on her forehead, and her face was smeared with pine tar, but her cheeks, flushed with effort, the graceful attitude of her limbs on the ground, and particularly her large dark eyes, which even in defeat were fearless and hopeful, made him think he had never encountered a more bewitching girl. Yet it was out of the question for him to think of her in that way. In fact, if he did not get her back to Oakhaven before night, she would be compromised. He cursed himself for not having insisted that a servant accompany them, as of course was proper. It was just that when he was thinking of Claire, what was proper did not seem to matter so much.

"Get up!" he said sharply. To get up was quite beyond Claire's strength even had she cared to obey. She simply turned over and hid her face in her arms. George picked up his ward by the back of her jacket, and half-carried, half-pushed her down into the quarry pit, which was now in deep shadow. There was a pool of clear water among the stones and George wet his handkerchief in it. "Wipe your face," he ordered, "you are dirty." He seemed to take in the dejected cleansing with an implacable regard. George longed to take Claire in his arms and comfort her, but he did not wish to horrify her again. And if he were to touch her, he was not sure he could bear to let her go. No, his feelings were wrong and would have to be endured.

"It's no use, sir. I cannot stay with you," she whispered, making him surer than ever that he was despised. He had to admire her courage in attempting to defy him, weak as she was, but he wasn't going to throw away his future just so she could go to the devil in her obstinate way.

"You have to," he said. "Do you think I take my obligations so lightly?"

Claire was glad that she was riding behind George so he could not see the tears flowing across her cheeks. Unexpectedly she lost consciousness, and her arms fell from the waist of his riding coat. George, feeling her grip slacken, reached behind him and broke her fall, nearly losing his own balance. It was now almost dark, and they were in a desolate spot. At the horizon, the sky was intense blue, and at the zenith George could already see the stars. "Poor little Claire," he whispered.

Lord Ross took his burden in his arms and rode

103

until he came to a rough inn he knew nearby. There Claire soon came to her senses. She was given a bowl of hot soup. Under the curious eyes of the other guests, George told her, "Eat, and do not dare to give me any more of your lip." Claire obeyed, and the food gave her strength. She had eaten nothing since the night before. She had to admire the economy with which George had put to rest the speculations of the other guests in the place. They were left to infer that she was a servant lad who had been knocked senseless for impertinence. George also had a bite of dinner and they continued their journey on two fresh horses. Hers was on a lead, which was humiliating, but she did not dare to say anything about it.

It was nearly midnight when they reached Oakhaven, where Wilson, Bennett, and Randall came out into the drive to meet them.

"Thank God," said Bennett.

"You wicked girl," scolded Randall. Claire was too sleepy to answer, so George reached up and lifted her down. The gentleness of his touch was so impossible, so sad, that Claire had to turn away to hide her tears. George turned to Wilson. "I shall go on Thursday to stay at Leland House, so send my things." Claire set off unsteadily for her room.

Behind her she could hear Wilson say, "She's a rude little thing. Not a word out of her."

George's voice followed, answering, "I wish I had never laid eyes on her, Wilson." Then she began to run, so as not to hear any more. Before she had summoned her courage to speak to him, before she had even conquered her weeping, George was off in his phaeton once more. He drove like the very devil, so he would not need to think of anything else.

When he arrived at Ashton Manor, Lady Patricia had not yet left for the ball. George came in tired but somehow elated, and gave her a friendly salute.

"La, Mr. Howard," she said, "I have never seen you look such a quiz. What is that black substance on your sleeve?"

Quartermayne, who was also nearby, quipped,

"The other ladies in the neighborhood must not be so particular."

"If you think I was courting a lady—" began George in an ugly tone of voice. Then he broke off, realizing that it might be better not to explain his movements. . . . "I had a problem at Oakhaven," he went on lamely, and went upstairs to change before the pine tar on his jacket could draw further comment.

That night at the ball, George became deplorably foxed, and fell downstairs, which was not at all like him.

Lady de Vere looked up as her brother entered the breakfast room. "I did not expect you up so early," she said tartly. "Last night you were as drunk as . . ." she cast about in her mind for an appropriate epithet ". . . as Lord Ross!" she concluded with satisfaction.

Desmarais ran his hand through his hair and groaned. "Do not tax me. If you knew what a head I have . . ."

"I do not understand George," mused Diana. "You are always watching him. Perhaps you can explain to me why he was so delightfully gay last August, when he had no prospects whatever, and now he is *quite* out of sorts."

"I do not suppose George would care to hear you say he is out of sorts." Viscount Desmarais took some food on his plate but did not eat it.

"Lord Ross is the most original man," went on his sister, "but I cannot see, now that he is getting everything he wanted, why he should jeopardize it all by making a cake of himself at the Ashtons'."

"A last-ditch defense," Desmarais said thoughtfully, "against marriage."

Diana was startled. "How can you say that? He adores Lady Patricia. I would have said at Oakhaven that she had him quite enslaved."

"Diana," said Desmarais patiently, with the air of someone explaining to a tiny child, "perhaps he does not wish to be 'enslaved' as you so aptly put it."

105

"But he was delighted to be able to offer for her."

"That was because he was excited over his title. But the way he acted at Ashton's was vile. He doesn't give a damn what people think," explained Desmarais with contempt.

"You are wrong about him there," considered Diana. "If he did not care for opinion, would he have worked so hard to hide his poverty? No, he would have emigrated, as I advised him to do. In America he could have become a rich man."

"And come home to marry the Lady Diana de Vere!" said her brother, wickedly.

"I shall put arsenic in your coffee!" countered Diana.

"I think someone must have done so last night," replied her brother, stretching his bony, tapered fingers across his pale brow with an expression of genuine pain.

Chapter 18

When Claire awoke the next morning, she found the door to her room locked. Ellen soon came up with a tray from the kitchen, closely followed by Randall, who gave her charge a severe dressing down for the trouble she had caused Lord Ross and the anxiety all the servants had suffered over her safety and her reputation. Then Bennett came in and removed the offending tweeds. "It is no point wasting good cloth," she said. "I'll put 'em in the sack for the parish. You ought to be ashamed, gallivantin' around in such!"

"I would burn them if I were you," said Randall dryly and left the room.

The dressing down Claire received from Randall was nothing to the one she subsequently gave herself. She scolded herself for having been such a fool as to suppose George would let his pleasure go before his duty. She should have realized he would consider it a duty to retrieve her. When he did appear, she should not have run away from him in fear. Besides making her seem a complete scatterbrain, her fear had insulted him, and she had seen that he was hurt by it. George Howard was a gentleman. He would never hurt a defenseless woman, and if he meant to be harsh with her now, it was no more than she merited for having insulted him so.

Claire was also ashamed of having fainted, a terribly weak and missish thing to do. Last but by no means least, she berated herself for not having had the countenance to explain. There was no excuse for silence when so much needed to be said—about Viscount Desmarais, and Bettina, and Lady Patricia. She told herself that it did not matter. Lord Ross was engaged to Lady Patricia, and engagements were not easily broken. Claire remembered the passion of their kiss, before they knew they were observed.

Claire was in love with George. She had wanted very badly to be taken up in his arms, but George had too much honor to give in to a whim of desire. She was an insignificant child, tied to him only by a crazy quirk of law—a child he believed to be disobedient, improper, and a wanton liar.

There was only one thing to do. Claire would have to write to him and apologize. His words came back to her with bitter force. *'Wretched brat . . . Come down out of that! . . . Do you think I take my obligations so lightly? . . . Wipe your face. You are dirty."*

In saying them over to herself she had to cry again. It was no use pretending that George could love her, but maybe he could forgive. At last Claire got out pen and paper to write her apology. Two hours later she had completed six closely written sheets and read them through with nausea. After several more attempts in the same vein, marked by slightly better spelling but no more propriety as to their content, Claire paused to open the window to feed the sparrows some crumbs from her tray. A strong gust of wind entered the room, sweeping the crumbs from the sill and the paper from the table. The paper eddied about the room and glanced against the wall as she hurried to close the casement. Then, shivering with a sudden chill, Claire collected and burned them all, and in the deep conviction that George would not care to be bothered with more, sat down to write her apology in the briefest possible terms:

My lord,
 I must apologize for my foolishness in supposing that you would allow me to leave your house. I will not make the same error in future.
 I must also beg your pardon for insulting your intended as I did. It was a rudeness to your friend, and therefore to you. It is possible that

Lady Patricia did not mean any harm by what she did.

Your penitent ward,
Claire Amberly

It is possible, thought Claire, but I am damned if it is likely. Although it was quite late, Claire called for Randall to take the sealed letter, so it could be posted in the morning. Soon she might receive a reply to it, and perhaps George might even come to Oakhaven. If he did, it would probably not be on her account, but she would see him nonetheless.

Claire had never allowed herself to be kissed, but she had heard the experience described in various and contradictory terms. I was a fool, she told herself. I should have offered myself to him while he was interested in me. Now I will probably never be on terms with him again. I suppose he's had hundreds of women. I wonder how my body would look to him after all those others?

Claire began to undress, slowly pulling off her shoes and stockings. Standing barefoot on the icy floor, she faced the long glass and removed her dress, her petticoat and her underwear. Her butchered hair stood about her head in unruly splendor. Her back was straight; her cheeks were flushed with imagination. George, she thought. If I were George, I wouldn't mind kissing *her*. Her breasts are round, her fingers are delicately tapered, her lips . . . Claire approached the glass, staring her image full in its stormy gray eyes. She leaned over and kissed the mirror and its cold hard surface came as a shock.

Suddenly she was naked and shivering with cold. The heat of her dream had been blown away as abruptly as the failed sheets of her letter had been whisked from the table. Hurriedly she dived for the covers of her bed and lay there overcome with shame. George must never know she had such thoughts and neither must anyone else. She lay in her bed for a long time without moving or making any sound.

●　　●　　●

Claire Amberly could not enjoy riding any of the Oakhaven hacks while Virgil languished in the stables at Leland House, or Ashton Manor, or wherever his master had seen fit to take him. She turned to walking instead to relieve the restlessness that often overcame her. When the weather was stormy, it seemed to help, as if the elements were in sympathy with her anger and loneliness. On one such day she returned to Oakhaven soaked but refreshed, hoping as usual to find that some communication had arrived from George Howard.

Although she knew from the gossip of Lady Buffington and Marianne Leland that Lord Ross was much sought after and would consequently be very busy in London, she thought that surely by now he would have answered her note. Up in her tower room Claire stared dumbly out the window, at the rain running down the glass, instead of changing to dry things, until Randall chanced to see her and administer a sharp reproof.

The next morning Claire was congested and feverish. For several days she was forced to keep to her bed. Although the girl's cold was not serious, Randall found Claire's apathy rather alarming. She wished neither to read nor to converse and lay passive while Randall carefully snipped her hair into some semblance of neatness, a procedure to which the housekeeper felt she never would have submitted if she had been herself. However, since Claire did not complain of pain or unhappiness, perhaps it was foolish to worry about her. Nevertheless, Randall gave the matter a casual mention in her regular letter to Lord Ross. She's too headstrong, thought the housekeeper, but I hate to see her so downhearted.

Having received no answer to her apology by post, Claire determined to write another more complete one, which included an explanation of what Lady Patricia and Bettina must have done. This apology, although polite, was colder and even less abject than her first. Claire knew very well that Lord Edward

110

would never have accepted either of them. This letter met the same fate as its predecessor.

Lady Patricia descended the stairs of Leland House daintily, a bit of the silk of her chastely cut morning frock held up to prevent her from tripping on her spiral course. As she did every day, Lady Patricia took the basket of mail for the ladies of the house and brought it upstairs to her desk to be sorted and answered if necessary. Her father's secretary had already removed the correspondence addressed to Lord Leland. Immediately she noticed another letter addressed to Lord Ross in a distinctive Italian hand. Carefully, she unsealed it with a hot knife, as her first ladies' maid had taught her to do. Perhaps, she thought, this letter will not have to be burned. If it is angry and defiant I will deliver it to him. Unfortunately, this letter was even less acceptable than the first. It contained a plausible guess as to her own role, if not her motives, and the language was polite and respectful. Lady Patricia dropped the letter into the fire, a fleeting smile crossing her delicately rouged lips as she did so. It would be best not to disturb Lord Ross's interest in the new life he was finding in town. A draught blew the letter off the fire, and Lady Patricia went after it with the tongs and was caught pushing it firmly between two logs as George came into the room.

Lady Patricia jumped at the sight of him, and nearly dropped the tongs. George offered to call a servant to fix the fire to her liking. "You should not soil your pretty hands with such work," he told her. Lady Patricia looked over to one side, distracted. George noticed then that a corner of a letter had been the object of her attention, and she saw his eye move to it.

With a shamefaced air she said, "I was cleaning out my desk—burning some old l-letters." George grinned. Let her burn her old love letters in peace. He thought indulgently that he had not known of her ever having been attached enough to treasure anyone's correspondence.

"I'm going out to see Pomfret's house. I will be back at four, for our excursion," he said, bending to kiss her hand in farewell. She pulled her fingers away. Patricia loved to have him kiss her hand in public, but when they were alone she was often impatient with him. He knew she did not wish him to buy Pomfret House, because it was not directly in contact with her current circle of friends. "Do not worry," he assured her, "I shall decide nothing without consulting you."

"See that you do not," she said with a false, arch smile, and then ran to him and gave him a quick perfunctory hug around the waist. He smiled at her slowly and went out.

When he had left the room, Lady Patricia realized that her ears were burning. It was all right. George obviously thought her actions were quite innocent, but thank God he had not entered the room a moment sooner! George was almost too easy to manage most of the time. It was simple enough to remain always a little bit out of his reach. Soon they would be the most fashionable couple in town. Patricia was still determined that she could persuade George to buy Morson House near Regent's Park. Even though the place was priced a bit high for him to afford without her assistance, it was worth the expense to be at the nerve center of the ton.

That evening, at the gala celebration the duke was giving in honor of Guy Fawkes Day, she felt that surely she could get George into exactly the right mood to acquiesce. There was to be an amateur theatrical performance, in which Quartermayne had a small part, which promised to be hilarious, a supper of the most elegant kind, and a display of fireworks unequaled since before the war. Best of all, there was to be no dancing. Lady Patricia had noticed that George was never in a perfect humor after he had danced, and it was imperative that he should be in the best of spirits to agree to reside in a house that he thought suited him so ill. Lady Patricia found herself lost in a reverie, imagining him in wedding clothes. They would suit him ill, too, she decided. In fact,

112

George might be at his best without any. He was the only man she had ever been acquainted with who had the power to make her heart beat faster, the only man it thrilled her to touch. Her father was hateful to make her wait to have him.

Lord Ross had finally got his business affairs in order and settled his various debts, without (he hoped) calling attention to their magnitude. He was now able to indulge freely in the pursuit of pleasure without the nagging concern for finance that had plagued his existence hitherto. He could now box or hunt or race phaetons without concern for cost or time, other than that required for rendering services to Patricia. She often asked for his presence at times when it was cursed inconvenient. There were also times, although not very often, when she treated him with such flippancy and unconcern that he was brought to wonder why she had asked for his attendance in the first place.

Lord Leland was pleased to observe that young Lord Ross had nearly abandoned the practice of gambling, which had formerly seemed such a passion with him. Now George went only occasionally to his club, and did not visit the wilder hells at all. Lord Leland could not guess the relief with which George had desisted from his former means of support. Unfortunately, George was having trouble finding an occupation with which to replace all his financial machinations. The reason he felt so dull was partially because it was no longer really necessary to expend his efforts on anything.

That morning Desmarais had asked George if he intended to bring his ward to town, and it had brought all his thoughts of Claire to his brain again. He had tried with some success to forget about her, for a number of excellent reasons. The strongest of these was that he found Claire's behavior strange. The inappropriateness and unacceptability of her actions made him fear his ward might be mad. Her upbringing had begun in hardship and continued in cruel

113

neglect, and his handling of her had not helped matters, judging from the results. It was appalling to him to contemplate Claire's brilliant mind and sensitive spirit lost to madness. The worst of it was that if she were truly to lose her reason, he would still be her guardian, and he and Patricia would have to see to her care all her life.

George's second reason for attempting to forget Claire was that he still wanted her, and this made him feel guilty not only for entertaining such wrong feelings toward his ward, but for lack of loyalty to Lady Patricia. George had given Patricia his word, and although he had not yet been permitted to make his offer formally, he felt his promise was as binding an obligation as if it had been announced in the *Gazette*. His third, and least important reason was annoyance with Claire for failing to write to him to explain her conduct. On the return trip to Oakhaven after her atrocious escapade, he had admired her restraint in sparing him the hysterics he feared and despised. Still, he could not help feeling that she owed him an apology.

Chapter 19

Imprisoned as she was by fever and the weakness that followed, Claire lay thinking. It was as if all the elements in her life were reduced to one compelling idea—Lord Ross—and all the remnants of her former preoccupations swept around it and were sucked away like leaves in the vortex of a whirlpool. It was no use being angry with herself for wanting what she had known she could never have: his love. She was not sorry she had given him hers. When Penthwaite had called her perverse and stubborn, her companion had been right. Was it perversity that had made her fall in love so hard and so impossibly?

The relationship she had with Lord Ross was one of guardian to ward, and like a warder in a prison, he was bound by his role. Claire had first thought of leaving Oakhaven in anger, at the time of Edward's death, and had attempted it in anger the time George had brought her back. Now she considered it more calmly and with hope. From the point of view of material comfort, leaving would be a disaster. Still, comfort at Oakhaven could never bring her happiness. George Howard had had the courage to climb those ladders at Badajoz, knowing almost certainly that he would be thrown down. She should at least have the courage to live without comforts in order to free herself from this obsession.

Everything and everyone at Oakhaven belonged to George—good George, who did not deserve to have her anger directed at him simply because fate had made her his problem. When she was no longer an unwanted nuisance in his life, perhaps he would remember her more kindly, and if they ever met on equal terms . . . No, it was no use supposing that George would not resent her defection; he had been angry enough at her for trying it before. She could not pretend he would receive her after she had carried out her plan, but if no letter came, it could only be a sign that he wished to be done with her.

It was almost winter. Already the roads were hard going, and frost had touched the fields at dawn. It was a bad time to leave, but Claire knew that George would marry soon, and she would rather die than stay after that. Lady Patricia had shown herself to be an enemy clever enough to detect the love Claire thought she had concealed so well and ruthless enough to act without compunction to destroy it. It had all been so unnecessary. I am too young and insignificant to attract George anyway, Claire thought. I won't come out in London, although I can go there. I can go anywhere I want to go. It was a thrilling, if not entirely welcome thought.

After regaining her health, Claire walked to the post daily, but no letter came. George had left his desk unlocked when he departed, and in it Claire had found an old seal ring which had belonged to George's father, and a sample of George's signature. After practicing for hours Claire was able to produce an inferior copy, and over it she wrote a letter to herself in a neat round hand such as Jarvis affected.

Claire visited the bookstore in the village, where she sold her book of Italian gardens for a fraction of its value and hired the clerk to post her letter when he went up to London. Afterward, she retrieved her boy's clothing from the parish sack, replacing it with a bulky skirt she no longer wanted. She was then ready to depart for London.

Her letter did not arrive at Oakhaven until Monday the eighteenth. Claire opened it immediately and stood quietly reading. Although no one was nearby, she reviewed her handiwork: "London, November 12 [it read] Dear Claire, I have found a chaperone who will tolerate you. In order to take up residence with

116

her you are to come [Edward would have said 'I require you to come'] to London on Tues. the nineteenth. Have Hawkins drive you in whichever rig suits him best. Stop at the Black Swan. [This was where Claire had stayed with Lord Edward on their return from Italy. It was the only hotel name she knew in London.] I will be in the neighborhood, and can escort you best from there. We can discuss your letters to me at that time. [Claire had made this part deliberately cold, and the whole letter rushed and abrupt, so the servants would excuse its writer for such obvious omissions as the name of the chaperone.] As I do not suppose you have much money, Randall will advance you the necessary. I do hope your health is well enough established so that the journey will not be a hardship. Yours, etc. Geo. L. Howard." (Here again she had debated as to whether she should sign him simply Ross, which certainly would have been easier to forge. In the end she had decided that the longer form was more characteristic. She loved the large *G* and the little *eo* that followed it, and the unique, backhanded curling *L* for his mother's maiden name that was always included on the letters she had seen.)

Trembling with guilt and apprehension, Claire took the letter to the servants' hall.

"I declare, Miss Amberly," ejaculated Randall after she had read it, "it's just like him to be so high-handed! One day is all we have to get you ready!"

"It does not matter, Randall," said Claire, trying to subdue her trembling, "I can bring the dirty things up in a laundry bag, or leave them here."

"That you shall not!" insisted Randall, and launched the household into a frenzy of preparation.

The trip to London was uneventful if uncomfortable. The roads were bad, but Hawkins handled the rig very well. At the Black Swan, Hawkins, who had been put in charge of the money, paid for Claire's room. He departed reluctantly when Claire produced a message from Lord Ross to the effect that that was what he should do. Hawkins could not read, and had a trusting nature, but he did not feel right about

117

abandoning his charge. Claire felt a surge of tenderness at his parting smile. Hawkins and Bennett, ignorant as they were, were the only real friends she had. The coachman would take the brunt of Lord Ross's wrath when he found out how easily Claire had duped them.

Instead of ordering supper, Claire began her economies by finishing the cold picnic Randall had prepared. She found that she could not sleep; the city seemed so noisy. Odd sounds kept jolting her into apprehension. Unreasonably, she imagined that her guardian would appear as the false message she had written said he would do, and guilty thoughts ran through her mind. At the earliest opportunity Claire left the hotel, dressed in her dusty heliotrope dress and hooded cape, and carrying her boy's clothing and as many other necessities as would fit into the cloak-bag.

The city was bewildering, but at last Claire was able to locate herself on the map she had torn from one of Edward's old books. After breakfasting at a small restaurant near the common stage, she obtained the names and addresses of three inexpensive hotels. The first would not take her because of her looks, but the second, a lot dirtier, was ready enough when she said she would pay for the week in advance—bed and breakfast. The five-pound note was finally changed.

The next day Claire's attack on the registries was unsuccessful. Clerks and secretaries were generally of the male sex. Governesses taught French and the pianoforte. Ladies' maids could dress hair, and all had to have character references. The registry employees took a dim view of Claire's cropped hair and hotel address. They suspected that they were dealing with a runaway blue blood, and wanted no part of her.

By the end of Saturday, Claire's dress was hopelessly soiled, and she had to resort to her boy's outfit while it was washed and pressed. In trousers and jacket she felt somehow invisible, and her fear abated, although things were not going well. She would have to find still cheaper accommodations or give up eating.

On Monday Claire looked for work as a salesperson in a number of haberdashery shops. She demonstrated that she could write, cipher, speak French and Italian, and do invoices. Unfortunately the only place with a position open was with a man whose major interest was to undress his employee. After evading him for all of Tuesday, Claire decided that the position would not do.

On Wednesday morning Claire arranged to sell her blue dress and long wool cape for enough money to afford her a week's lodging in a boarding house near Covent Garden. Dressed in her tweeds, she delivered the things the same day. For the first time, Claire regretted never having asked Lord Edward Ross for any jewelery or trinkets. Even a tiny gold ring or a single pearl would have come in handy now—but Claire had always asked for books.

Chapter 20

It was Friday, and dark already, but the sparrows were still fluttering and swooping around their ivy-covered homes in the church eaves. Claire could stand on the street corner now without a trace of fear. She had at last rid herself of the gripping feeling of waiting, of being followed and observed. Calmly she removed her handkerchief from the pocket of her jacket and blew her nose with it. The handkerchief was trimmed with fine lace. Claire had found it that morning on the sidewalk in front of the theater, a good way from where she was now standing. God knew how many miles she had walked, and it must have been God who had led her a week before, to follow the sound of the choir into St. Anthony's Church. After she had rested through the service in comfort, she had listened to the people speaking to the priest and observed that he was an Italian. After waiting in the shelter of the pew while the faithful went in and out of the confessional, she had had an idea which led her to do likewise.

Father Giovanni had been surprised at hearing so fair an urchin speak to him in flawless Italian. "Father, I have not been to confession in over four years," he began. "There was no Roman church where I have lived, but only the Anglican. . . . I have disobeyed the man set in authority over me and have run away from his house."

"You are referring to your father, or your stepfather?" asked the priest.

"I am referring to my guardian's younger brother, who was put in charge of me by his brother's will. My own parents are dead. My guardian is only ten years older than I am. It was impossible for me to stay there, so I put on boy's clothing and came away."

Father Giovanni started. From the way his penitent had looked, he would not have guessed she was female. "I compliment you," he answered. "Your disguise is good, but don't you know it is a sin?"

"I know it, Father, but it is a sin that came easily to me. When I was small, my father dressed me in trousers and sent me to a boys' school so I could learn Latin. It was a choir school—Sant'Angelo in Ravenna. When I heard your choir sing, it made me want to confess. . . ."

"Then you must do so," Father Giovanni was a little flustered. He did not quite know what he should tell this transvestite. "Why did you leave your guardian? Did he behave improperly to you?" he temporized.

"No, Father. I behaved improperly to him. I fell in love with him and that was wrong, because he was engaged to marry an earl's daughter. She hated me on sight and tricked him into hating me, too. Now that I have run away, he would never take me back. He believes I am bad, but I am not. I wish to make my own way, but I have no trade. If you would let me sing in your choir, only for a few weeks, I could stay alive long enough to find honest work." Father Giovanni looked at her through a crack in the grille of the confessional. Her long lashes were cast down modestly. Apparently she did not care to try the obvious trade open to girls of her kind. Certainly she was good-looking enough. It seemed a shame to send this rare packet of beauty and virtue away to pay for her sins in this traditional way. He had seen too many girls follow that all but inevitable path and it angered him.

"How old are you?" he asked her.

"Sixteen, Father." She thought him much more likely to take her as a singer if she said she were younger than she was.

"Too old, too old," he said sadly. "The other priests would hear the difference. But I have an idea. Could you serve as an acolyte?"

"Oh, yes, Father." So it had been settled. She could

121

earn a shilling a week serving at early morning service, and again at evensong, and in exchange had to promise to put off boy's clothing as soon as she had found a safe place to stay. Claire had turned up for services promptly, and had worked well, although hunger and the incense sometimes made her feel faint. Now she stood outside the church with her shilling in her pocket, feeling no worry more grave than the trouble of deciding which shop to enter to get something to eat. The sparrows were making a great noise in the ivy under the church eaves. Claire put her hand in her pocket to make sure the shilling was still there. When she had touched it, she felt beside it the weathered contour of the glass king's face: the only object that remained to remind her of the past.

Suddenly, she was jerked back into the alley by a hand on the back of her jacket. She could not see her assailants, so hard was her nose pressed against the bricks. A strong hand twisted her arm behind her and other hands entered her pockets. Claire smothered her scream of revulsion, as she had no wish to be left bleeding on the cobblestones. Then, as quickly as they had come, the thieves were gone back into the shadows. All Claire had been able to see was that one of them had had a rather wide face, and a fur collar on his cape. She thought she might know him again. Claire was a little dazed. Her money was gone—the shilling and the two coppers so was her handkerchief and comb, but the thieves had tossed aside the gothic glass as worthless. Claire picked it up out of the mud and washed it in a nearby rain barrel.

After washing her hands, Claire began to move aimlessly, passing the shop where she had pawned her blue dress, hardly seeing anything around her as she struggled with the realization that she could not eat or sleep as she had planned. It was hard. From a number of inns emerged puffs of warm air perfumed with cookery. She had waited so long—she could almost cry but there was no point with nobody to sympathize. She went around to the back of the Pig and Chicken to see if perhaps the cook might be persuaded to let her work for a meal, but the scullions said the cook was busy, and would not let her in. While she was attempting to change their minds, an old woman came up and began rummaging through some garbage that had been thrown out. One of the lads ran out and threw dishwater on her, and she retreated, screaming oaths. Claire listened with attention. This was English the likes of none she had ever heard.

Sadly Claire walked on and turned by chance toward the Thames. It was better to keep moving so as to feel less chill. It would also be best to go to a part of town where people ate in dining rooms—not out in the street where she could watch them. The sky was blackening, but clouds and smoke hid any stars there may have been. Claire picked up a stick, walked with it for a while, and then threw it into the river, watching it fetch up in the filthy swirl flowing past the starlings under London Bridge. After a little, the carts and hacks began to be mixed with the vehicles of the quality, and now and then Claire spied a chair being carried along the street. She had never ridden in a chair. She preferred to appraise the horses going by, distinguishing the blooded ones from the commoners. Many were definitely worth looking at, and must have cost a long price, but none struck her as being quite as fine as Virgil. Thinking about the horses made her feel, however briefly, like a person of superior judgment.

Suddenly Claire remembered that Hawkins owed her two bob, for a wager they had made on Virgil's ability to take a certain hedge. He had never paid. If Lord Ross were staying at Leland House, it was possible that Hawkins was there with him. It occurred to her that if she could contrive to see the coachman alone she could collect the money and not be caught. She had fooled him often enough before. She smiled to think what he would say about her clothes. Collins was the one to avoid, but he was so diffident, so far above the other servants, that it might well be possible to see Hawkins without drawing his notice.

Claire began to inquire of various persons the

direction of Leland House. She remembered dimly
that someone had said it faced on St. James's Park.

In this section of town Claire felt dirty and out of
place. Approaching from the other side of the park,
she peered at the row of clean imposing fronts. It was
much too dark already to read the nameplates from
that distance, but Claire felt she could guess which
door the Lelands' must be. Flanked by carved pilas-
ters and antique statuary, it was by far the most elegant entrance of them all. Coming closer, she verified
her guess. As she stood hesitating before the bell, a
lady's carriage stopped next door, and its occupant
fixed her with such a baleful glance that Claire
paused, and retreated across the street in confusion.

Now Claire told herself that it would be foolish to
knock at the servants' entrance on the off chance that
Hawkins would be there. It had been stupid of her to
think she might approach him discreetly. Hawkins
was probably back at Oakhaven, and if Collins or
Anne were to see her, it would be all up. Claire could
not bear the thought that Lady Patricia or her servants should see her in boy's clothing. Even if Hawkins were there, he would probably haul her before his
master immediately. Claire turned abruptly and
walked back toward the river, the image of the house
with its lighted windows and beautiful carved door
still before her eyes. No wonder George had wanted
to stay there.

By the time Claire reached the market area where
she knew at least the names of the streets, she was
very tired and more miserably hungry than before.
Fog was starting to rise off the river, and the damp
air lay stagnant and chill across the city. As Claire
stood and watched the men and women going in and
out of the public houses, and saw waifs more ragged
than herself huddled in doorways or attempting to
beg, she felt she could not bear another hungry night.

On every corner there were carts, selling hot things
to eat, catering to the traders who patronized the great
vegetable market. One man in particular was doing a
brisk trade in sausage rolls. After watching him for a
few moments, Claire reached nimbly between two

customers to grab one. Quick as she was, the vendor was quicker. He leaped out from behind his counter and grabbed her arm before she could get past the people on the street corner. He jerked her toward him so roughly that the sausage went flying into the dirt. Then the vendor hauled Claire over to his cart, and before she could see what he was about, pressed her hand down on the grill of his brazier. Claire screamed and he flung her from him into the street. A carter narrowly missed her as she rose and stumbled into a nearby alley amid the jeers of the customers and general street noise.

Gasping with pain, Claire thrust her hand into the mud to cool it and creeping to the blind end of the alley, huddled there on a loose stone. Moisture dripped down the bricks near her head but no wind disturbed the air. "Oh," Claire whispered desperately to herself, "oh, oh." She kept as still as possible so as to attract no further notice and nursed her hand. She could not see how bad it was. Then the remaining light dimmed, and Claire looked up to see the black silhouette of a broad-shouldered boy between her and the street. In one motion Claire stood up, seizing a loose brick with her good hand and placing her back to the wall.

"I have no money," she breathed. "You are wasting your time."

"'d be a poor man'd rob such as you!" sneered the lad. "While 'e was tendin' t' you, me 'n me mate copped three a these buns 'n I tho't you c'd 'ave one 'cos 'twas you as got burnt."

Although she was by no means sure she had understood what he had said, Claire could see that he was holding something out to her. She reached for it with her hurt hand and nearly dropped it. Letting the brick fall to the ground, Claire looked at the roll in disbelief. "Thank God," she sputtered and began to eat.

"Y'd do better t' thank me," grumbled her benefactor. "Green as grass you must be t' try t' rip off old Ned. There may be no watch 'ereabout, but 'e does well enough. Burnt me once, too, when I was a nip-

125

per. Well. No mind . . ." his voice trailed off as he began to withdraw from the alley.

"Thank you," she said at last. "You are right. I never stole anything before. It was good of you. . . ." Claire raised her sleeve in an unsuccessful attempt to wipe off the mud and tears.

"'d I see you at St. Anthony's?" asked the youth. Claire nodded, her mouth full. "Wot's yer name?"

"Carl Andrews," she lied nervously, flexing her burned hand.

"'r they after you f'r aught?" asked the lad. "Me name's Will. Wooly Will, they says sometimes, 'cos me hair curls so tight."

"Nobody is after me, Will," she said cautiously, squinting at his soiled brown mop in the bad light. "I ran away from my master."

"'r you bound t' 'm?" asked Will.

"No. But he was unkind to me and called me a liar." Suddenly, despite herself, Claire began to sob. "Now I have no place to go, at all."

"You must be a damned fool. What were you, a clerk? You talk like a clerk."

"I was . . . a stable boy. I talk this way because I was taught to. I know it was stupid to run away but I had to do it."

"Who was yer master?" Will looked closely at his new acquaintance. "Better t' take a lammin' than lose a good place—to my mind." Claire's eyes were so fearful that he could see it was no use to press for more information. "No need t' say, then. Get on wi' no master, meself," he concluded.

"He'd never take me back now," she told him. It was true. After what she had done, she should never be received by George Howard or any other member of society. She had disgraced herself too thoroughly for that. Claire stood up and prepared to be on her way.

Wooly Will looked over his find. It was possible he might be able to put this lad to use. Since Tom was in Newgate and Ben taken by the press, his gang had done little of any value. They wanted new blood, and a needy green lad would do as he was told.

"Ye c'n kip in wi' me, come daylight," he offered, "if you find some wood f'r the fire. I'll show you where t' bring it. Me mother 'n me brother 'ave the bed nights," he explained.

Claire could only wonder at a family so poor that they had to sleep in shifts, but she was glad of any plan, any hope of respite from the cold. Meekly she nodded her head and followed Wooly Will to where she was to meet him at daybreak.

Before morning came Claire would have been glad of the stick she had thrown into the Thames. She had found so little wood that she feared it would never satisfy Will. The few dead branches she had pulled off trees in the churchyard, and the broken crate left by a carter would not even heat a single room. The best piece she had was a hardwood chair seat. When Will finally arrived, wearily dragging his feet, however, he was not displeased. He opened the door to the place and made a small fire for his mother's coffee. Then without ceremony he hauled both of his relatives out of bed and pointed at the side where he wanted his new friend to lie. After removing her shoes and pulling the covers up to her neck, Claire fell asleep instantly.

Will's mother, Mrs. Burke, regarded the interloper with little interest. This was not the first individual her son had entertained in this style. She hoped, at least that this one was not infested with the worst sorts of vermin. Poor as she was, Mrs. Burke had a horror of "crawlers." Coughing fitfully, she turned to the pile of wood. It was nice to know that at least she would be able to heat the food.

Awake at last, her son Tony, a boy of nine, bent over the grimy creature who had displaced him. "I know 'im," said the lad, looking at Will, "ain't 'e the one who serves at evensong?" Will said nothing. He was carefully wiping his boots. "At St. Anthony's, I mean, where I sing?" insisted Tony. Will nodded, swinging his huge feet up and under the covers. " 'e never says nothin'. Too 'igh 'n mighty, 'e is!" went on the lad.

"Shut yer face, Tony," said Will, good-naturedly,

closing his eyes. "Who wouldn't be 'igh 'n mighty wi' the likes of you?" Tony went over to the table, out of range of instant retaliation, and made an awful face at his brother, but Will did not see it.

The following night at White's, Dr. Westgate, who was in London on one of his routine trips to obtain medical supplies, ran into Lord Ashton and engaged him in a desultory game of gin, for the usual stakes.

"Do you know, I missed your ball for nothing," observed Westgate as his friend dealt out the cards. "Lady Stanwich never sent for me. It was all a hum. Damned if I can figure out why anyone would want me drawn off. No one died of poisoning at your place, did they?" he asked lightly.

"No. Not a soul. Ross got drunk and fell downstairs. Had a dreadful row with his ward right after you left. I never heard what it was all about."

Doctor Westgate picked up the trey of hearts. "It has me at point non plus," he said.

"Oh, someone's jealous of you." Edward grinned at the idea of Westgate, who was in his early fifties, inspiring jealousy. He discarded the queen of diamonds.

Westgate remembered his ride with Lady Patricia and her cryptic remarks to him on that occasion. The ghastly possibility that George had written the note crossed his mind but was at once dismissed. He would recognize George's left-handed scrawl anywhere. Westgate remembered the short letters his godson had sent him from Winchester School, and later on, from Cambridge. No. George could never be that indirect. If he had found my conduct offensive, he would have told me to my face to get out. Westgate drew another spade, which did him no good whatever. "Have you seen Ross?" he asked his partner.

"He was not at Lady Pendleton's ball?"

"Pendleton does not receive him."

"Oh, I forgot," returned Ashton, discarding his ace of clubs. "He and Sophia . . ."

"She was a fool to tell her mother. At that point

128

there was nothing to it but talk." The doctor picked up the ace.

"Oh, well," replied Ashton, "I suppose all young girls are fools."

"Around George Howard they are," returned the doctor, thinking of Alice Buffington in particular.

"Gin," said Ashton.

Chapter 21

Claire Amberly could well have slept for twenty-four hours, but at five that evening she was shaken roughly awake and immediately sent off to evensong. As she and Tony left the house, Mrs. Burke was sinking relievedly into the bed, and Will was brewing a bit of coffee with what was left of the wood. Claire had difficulty remembering the way back, so it was fortunate that Tony was with her. When they entered, she thought she had the wrong house and drew back. The room was full of people.

"You took yer bleedin' time," said Will. "Don't just stand there gawpin'! Shut the door!"

Hanging about near the stove, which still gave out a little heat, were Weezer, a redhead about five feet tall, very wiry and tough despite his short stature, and who already had a distinct moustache, and David, a tall Hasidic Jew who had just come from studying the Talmud. A bit apart from them was Clem, a beefy and rather handsome boy, who lounged near the sooty window pulling nervously at his decayed greenish cap. Eyeing him was Lucy, who sat straddling the only chair in the room in a most unladylike and artless manner. Tony, who had already supped, got into bed beside his mother.

Will handed Claire a plate of eggs, badly cooked in sausage drippings. She began to eat the cold eggs in silence, while she listened to them discuss the evening's plans. Lucy could not stay because she had to help her pa, who was cook at the Pig and Chicken.

It appeared that Will was the group's leader by virtue of his skill as a vegetable buyer. His father, a gardener, had taught him what he knew. Will bought with the money that was staked to him by members of the gang, and sold in the large nightly vegetable market. His choice was good, and usually some grocer would buy his whole stock at a fair price. The profit, however, was never enough to live on because there was little to invest. The money was divided scrupulously in proportion to the investment each person had made. On that first evening "Carl" showed her worth by working out the amounts rapidly, in her head.

All of them were rather free with comradely slaps and punches, which they exchanged in a desultory manner on meeting. Carl was much laughed at, until she began to punch back, and it was not many days before Will observed his protégée sailing into an encounter with fists at the ready.

Another of their steady activities was robbery, although Claire did not find this out at first. Lucy was often able to abscond with articles of clothing from the inn, and these were turned into money by David, the only member of the group who worked by day. His father kept a shop where second-hand clothing was sold.

Weezer had recently come up with a sound plan to acquire hats, and for a number of nights it had gone without a hitch. Men would come out of the gambling hell in Farringdon Street and cut down the alley to the stable, instead of taking the long way around the block. A piece of dark string tied across the alley at just the right height knocked the hats off, and Weezer would jump out a cellar window alcove and disappear with them. Will and Clem, appearing to stroll across the street before the gambling establishment, would block pursuit; Weezer would stash his acquisition in Will's kitchen and return to the scene. A good evening could net as many as four hats, costing, when new, from seven shillings to as much as five pounds, depending on the wealth of the victim. They could be sold for about a fourth of their value, but the take had to be divided five ways. Unfortunately, Will refused to do it with a party of more

131

than two men, so they were forced to let a great many fine hats escape.

While the boys were engaged in this, Claire would spend her time gathering fuel, and occasionally made forays into the richer parts of town in search of saleable trash. Will had put it about that Carl could write, and she occasionally got work penning a letter for some adult acquaintance of his at a halfpenny a sheet. However, Will's brother Tony had a habit of stealing her writing paper to copy out his letters and draw pictures of hanged men, which hampered her efforts.

Often Claire would loiter about the stable to warn the boys if the watch happened to be nearby. Once, inside the stable, a blooded mare became very excited because rainwater was leaking on her head. She had kicked in one side of the stall and bit Joseph, the night man, when he tried to move her. It was Claire who had finally gentled her, with a blanket over her head and a smooth, practiced hand. After that Joseph would sometimes give the urchin a bit of currying to do, or have her in to hold horses on theater opening nights. Even a few hours work at decent wages made Claire feel hopeful.

Autumn wore into winter and the town prepared itself for Christmas. The nights became so cold that Claire and Will could hardly sleep. One Sunday during holy communion, Claire filched a heavy tiered cape from Westminster Abbey and spent all afternoon sewing it into a very satisfactory blanket, over the protests of Will, who wanted to sell it. After having done that she could hardly plead honesty when Weezer fell ill and had to be replaced as picker-up of hats. Will did not feel disposed to retrain Clem, who had had difficulty mastering the blocking operation. Tony was too young, and slept nights, so Carl was really the only possible choice. She had great misgivings at first, but the first three hats were ridiculously easy. The gambling hell patrons were altogether too foxed to resist it effectively.

It was about four in the morning, and they were beginning to think the action was over for the night, when a lone tall gentleman began to saunter unevenly toward the alley mouth, whistling *Come, Thou Almighty King*. Fog had risen from the river and was flowing about his knees. He seemed to lurch against it like someone walking in the current of a stream. Claire found herself saying the words of the hymn over in her mind:

> Come, thou incarnate word
> Chaos and darkness heard
> And took their flight. . . .

A particularly beautiful pair of Hessians flashed by, to the rhythm of his whistle, which was cut short as the man's cane swung up suddenly and connected with the string, knocking his hat off forward, instead of backward, the way it would have gone if the string had knocked it off. The hat fell so near his boots that Claire hesitated a precious instant before grabbing for it. Although the gentleman had clearly shot the cat, his reactions were excellent, and Claire felt the touch of his glove on her coat as she ran. She was unprepared for the loudness of his roar, and for the way he floored Will and Clem with one vicious sweep of his cane.

"Louts!" he shouted. "Get out of my way!" Clem screamed with pain and both boys got up from the cobbles and made off as fast as they could. Claire found her way blocked by the footman from the gambling club, who had most uncharacteristically ventured out into the street. Turning to run the other way, she had to pass the outraged gentleman. For the first time she saw his face and recognized Desmarais. Claire stood for a split second in awe, flung away the hat, and ran down the filthiest alley she could find. His property regained, Desmarais did not pursue her very far. Back in Will's room the boys stood waiting for her, as Clem was to deliver the hats to David's house. They were less than delighted to see her appear empty-handed.

"D'you mean I got welted f'r naught?" whined Clem.

"The 'at was a Baxter, no less! You snabbled it right

133

enough, I saw. Where is it?" demanded Will in a fierce whisper, so as not to wake his mother and brother. Claire picked up a few sticks of wood and went over to begin making a fire in the stove. "Answer me!" he insisted.

Claire considered telling them a plausible lie, as she doubted if either of them had seen her fling the hat away, but she decided against it. "I know the bloke. I was bewattled by seeing him again—afraid he'd get me."

" 'n wot if 'e did?" sneered Clem.

Claire did not answer and Will instantly noticed the trace of remembered fear in her expression. "Was that peevy cove yer master?" he inquired.

"No. His friend, Viscount Desmarais. I'm sorry he hit you," she said to Clem, rather insincerely.

"Oi must apollygise fer me frend the Viscount Demmyray!" mocked Clem viciously. Will laughed. His mother raised herself on one elbow.

"Whisht, will you?" she moaned. Clem struck at Claire and caught his fist up against the stick of wood she held in her hand.

"He's not my friend," she muttered.

Clem took the sack with the hats and limped to the door. "Damned if I'll go out with 'im again," he said to Will. " 'ad 'is dabblers on it, 'n let it go." Clem slammed out, leaving her to make the morning fire as usual. They breakfasted on sausage, bread, and tea, after which Claire and Tony walked to church. When she returned, Mrs. Burke was sweeping and Will was asleep. She felt grateful that he had not been more angry with her.

Chapter 22

Hawkins had been back from London for two days when Randall received a routine inquiry from Lord Ross about Miss Amberly's health, since he had "had no word from Oakhaven since she was taken cold." This prompted Randall to send Lord Ross the forged letter by the next post, together with an account of Claire's departure as detailed as their combined memories could make it.

Upon receipt of this, George was at first incredulous, but knowing Randall to be incapable of deception he was forced to accept it as truth, and with the knowledge of truth came fury. His cousin, Michael Howard, was to visit Oakhaven in January, and it was a certainty that his visit would be more than simply social. If he could show that George was not caring for his ward, Michael could break the will, and George knew Michael well enough to be certain he'd take the opportunity.

George cursed his ward, his cousin, and the Oakhaven servants with verve and imagination and went off across town to the Black Swan where he found a cold trail and a bill for the storage of Claire's trunk. The discovery that she had left her trunk behind meant one of three things. She had meant to reclaim it but had come to some misfortune; she had resumed masculine dress; or she would be supplied with clothing at her destination. George began to curse again, so vividly that the innkeeper offered to reduce his charges. The trunk itself posed a problem, as he did not want it sent either to Leland House or to Oakhaven. Were he to discover Claire's whereabouts, she would need her things. Abruptly George made a decision. He would buy Pomfret House after all. He would surprise Patricia by having it fixed up so elegantly that she would have to admit she was wrong in despising it, and meanwhile, he could store the trunk there.

George went to see Pomfret at once. On the way, he began seriously to think about his problem. He had spent a great deal in London on high living, his new coach, and expensive gifts for Patricia. If he could not find Claire, he could lose his inheritance and only his title would keep him from debtor's prison. He wondered bleakly if it would affect Claire's behavior if she knew. At last he decided that it would be best to return to Oakhaven in search of some clue to her whereabouts.

First assigning Collins to investigate the homes of everyone who could have befriended her—a list that included principally the members of the October house party, and enjoining him to keep his operations totally secret, George simply left town. On receiving his terse excuse, the Lady Patricia hid her pique very well, but she vowed to make him feel it when he returned to London.

The ride to Oakhaven was long and hard, as the roads were in worse than usual repair. It was raining again and the inn where George attempted to take refuge was so abominable that he soon left. He preferred to travel rapidly on horseback than to be jolted slowly over the potholes in a coach where he could be warm and dry in the company of his nasty thoughts.

Much later, with his long rangy form stretched out before the fire in the library at Oakhaven, his mud-spattered buckskins steaming, and his boot up on a footstool, George rested his body but forced his mind to work. Each of the servants from the newly arrived butler, Mr. Wilson, to the lowest scullery maid were interviewed.

Bennett, who was summoned before him last of all, blurted out, "You should change to dry clothes, my lord, you'll catch your death!"

George's brows joined in a scowl that made Bennett shake with apprehension. "I will catch my ward, if it is all the same to you," he said. "If you are shielding her—if you know where she is, you had best tell me now!"

Bennett flushed with anger at being so distrusted. "If you 'adn't been too 'igh and mighty to answer 'er letters, she might not 'ave run off at all!"

"What letters?" asked George, and the honest bewilderment in his tone made Bennett sorry for her anger. Briefly she recounted all she knew of the letters, and Claire's daily walks to the post.

"She walked?" Lord Ross was incredulous.

"After Virgil was gone she seemed to lose 'eart for riding, my lord."

"I never received any letters, Bennett. Do you suppose she came to London to communicate with me and fell on some misfortune?"

"No, my lord," said Bennett sadly, "I think she connived to lose 'awkins so she wouldn't 'ave to see you."

"Did she have any visitors?" asked George sharply.

"No, my lord, but going to the post every day she could 'ave . . ."

"Both sent letters and received them!" Bennett closed her mouth tightly as her master's angry shout cut her off, and resolved that he would have no help from her. If she had known where the poor child was, she would not have told.

George saw shock and disapproval on her broad transparent countenance and fought down his desire to swear. Bennett was a kind, although ignorant, woman for whom he had a great deal of regard, and it was unfair of him to burden her with his worst suspicions. Claire had willfully run away from Oakhaven. The very best of the possibilities that had gone through his mind—that she had eloped with some local youth, an outcome which would at least have the merit of solving his legal problems—did not please him much more than the worst . . . that his ward had taken leave of her wits and was wandering mad and uncared-for through the streets of one of the hardest cities in the world.

With difficulty George began a new line of ques-

137

tioning. "Bennett," he began, "has Miss Amberly ever deceived you before?"

Bennett hesitated. "She deceived Penthwaite, and I suppose she did fool me as well."

"Penthwaite was the companion, am I right? The one Randall held in such esteem?"

"Randall was took in by 'er airs, my lord, but I was not. Thought she was always right," said Bennett resentfully.

"She must have had a good deal in common with my brother," interjected George dryly, "but get to the point. How did Miss Claire deceive her?"

"After the scandal with young Robbie 'artley, Miss Dumbarton left 'er place, and the baron 'ired Missus Penthwaite to reform the child. Miss Amberly was wild, but she was a good girl, and she didn't deserve Penthwaite, who never let 'er 'ave a minute to 'erself. 'is lordship told us not to interfere: Penthwaite was to 'ave a free 'and, but there were times . . ."

"I am not interested in your excuses for her, Bennett," said George.

"One day Miss Amberly 'appened to overhear Penthwaite boasting to a friend that if 'er charge's behavior was enough improved by Christmas, Lord Ross would triple 'er salary. If 'e was not satisfied, she was to be dismissed. Miss Amberly never let on that she 'eard. From that day she minded Penthwaite like an angel and took all 'er scolds so meekly I thought she was ill. She spent hours at embroidery so she'd be allowed to ride. But when 'is lordship came 'ome for Christmas, the chit wiped 'er fingers on 'er skirt, used cant words, and behaved as if Penthwaite was an old darling who indulged 'er. I'll never forget Missus Penthwaite's face when 'is lordship dismissed 'er." Bennett suppressed a smile. "After Missus Penthwaite was gone, Miss Amberly broke down and told Sir Edward what she 'ad done, and for once 'e didn't punish 'er. All 'e said was, 'e was damned if 'e'd spend a brass farthing on a governess again."

If what Bennett said were true, Miss Amberly's innocence was nothing but a front for the practiced, calculating liar she was. George remembered her deliberate rudeness to him, when she told him she hoped to be sent away, she could not say where. Now she had gone, and besides her rudeness there were other memories—her shyness, her cropped curls, the paths of tears across her dirty face. Had all that been a lie, too? George found himself suddenly unable to speak. He dismissed Bennett with a wave of his hand.

Next morning, George forced himself to search the neighborhood for clues. He traced the book of Italian gardens but learned nothing from its owner. He even rode up to the old ruined church.

George could not help remembering the day when he and Patricia had discovered Claire's retreat. Now winter had blasted the flowering weeds and the ruddy vines lay twisted and blackened by frost. Dry leaves still clung to a few of the stubbornest oaks, and the sky, which had then coursed with fluffy gray clouds now seemed made of frozen lead.

George remembered the glass king and searched for him under the dry leaves, recalling Claire's modest words, "I like it better than anything I can make with a needle." However, when the leaves had been brushed away George saw nothing but scattered shards of glass where the king had been.

Why? he asked himself. Why did Claire run away to London? Why had he not received her letters? Why had she been so headstrong and foolhardy? And the hardest question of all: Why does it make me so miserable? George scuffed among the ruins with the toe of his boot, looking for the king's face. He knew it was no use staying at Oakhaven any longer. If Claire could do this, she did not intend to come back.

From Oakhaven George set out to follow the only other lead he had. He hardly remembered Bettina; certainly he had never troubled to discover what she was really like. Her commonness had been good camouflage. Randall's words in telling of her dismissal had stuck in his mind. When Bettina had asked for a character Claire had said, "Get one from your other mistress." Randall had thought a former mistress was

139

meant, but to George it was clear that Claire believed Bettina to be employed by someone else—the person who had sent the maid to Oakhaven in the first place, the person she had accused of being a lying bitch: in a word, Lady Patricia. George had thought that Lady Patricia had taken no interest in his ward, malicious or otherwise. He might almost have preferred if she had. Probably Claire had dismissed Bettina because the maid had not helped her mask her disobedience, but before this quarrel Claire had genuinely liked her abigail.

George obtained the maid's direction from Bennett. She had indeed got a character from somewhere and had obtained a place in Lord Pendleton's London house. That's perfect, thought George. Pendleton does not receive me. . . . Bennett also told her master that Bettina had corresponded regularly with Lady Patricia's maid, Anne, and that it was surprising that when Anne came down to Oakhaven with her mistress, she behaved as if Bettina didn't exist. George determined to get to the bottom of the business as soon as possible, and sent the hapless Hawkins to arrange a meeting with Bettina on neutral ground.

Bettina was a bit appalled at the prospect of an interview with her former employer, and until George had given her the most strict assurances that their conversation would be perfectly confidential, she would not consent to speak to him.

George could tell at once by her guilty, defiant bearing that Bettina had something to hide. Looking into her dark, pretty eyes, he told her what had happened to Claire and watched those eyes fill slowly with tears of remorse. Succumbing, as many women had before her, to George's charm and authority, she found herself relating what she had sworn never to reveal. What she said was so fantastic that George hesitated to believe it. Just the same, there she stood, wiping away genuine tears with his handkerchief. Besides, it explained the doctor's hurried departure, and one of the things that had bothered him most— Claire's action in showing him her riding habit.

Bettina looked up at her former master's face. The

scar on his cheek had turned bright red, and his eyes, staring unseeing across the room, were so ferocious that Bettina was hard put to keep herself from bolting.

It was a bitter shock to George to have so mistaken Lady Patricia's character. He had thought she was so honorable, so decorous, so sure of herself. Yet if Bettina were to be believed, Lady Patricia had engaged in an improper escapade, apparently for no other cause than jealousy—or perhaps not even jealousy, since Patricia had little cause to be jealous of a girl who disliked and avoided her guardian. It must have been done for pure malice, and more to manipulate him than to discredit Claire.

"I'm sorry," Bettina had told him, "Lady Patricia told me she dressed up as Claire to make Viscount Desmarais jealous of Dr. Westgate." George shook his head.

"I guess you will think twice before meddling in your employers' affairs from now on," he said.

"Oh, my lord, I never would! If I hadn't needed her to give me a character, I would never have spoken to Lady Patricia again, for she bubbled me, too! Oh, please do not tell her that I talked!" George promised seriously not to, but entreated Bettina to help him find his ward. Unfortunately, Bettina was as ignorant of Claire's whereabouts as he was and could give him no useful help.

George could not confront Lady Patricia with Bettina's story without exposing his informant, and he felt that he had been gravely wrong in going off half-cocked when this nonsensical business began to be bothersome. If only he had been calmer then, perhaps it could have been sorted out without all this pain. This time, he determined to be ruled by his brain, but in the hours that followed he found it far from easy to hold to this resolve.

Chapter 23

Gloom hung over the city. Puddles from the recent rain lay steaming up into the mist. George went to his new house to change. He did not wish to appear at less than his best before Patricia. Collins did not care at all for his master's mood, but was much too wise to say so. It was not at all an appropriate mood for morning calls—particularly not calls to a lady a man held in affection.

The new carriage moved at a snail's pace through the fog-bound streets, as the coachman feared a collision that would mar the shining surface of the vehicle. George was glad of the delay, as the fog in the streets was nothing to the murk that befouled his will, blocking his ability to plan the encounter that lay before him. He must appear to be duped. God, what a fool she must think me, he mused, and it's no more than I deserve. He wondered briefly if Lady Patricia could possibly respect a husband who was so gullible. No, he decided. If she had really done this, it showed contempt for him, a clear disregard for propriety, and a deviousness of mind he found hard to imagine—a deviousness that could easily defend itself unless caught unawares. Thinking back to the day this deception was supposed to have happened, George remembered dimly that Lady Patricia had been flushed and vivid, just as she had been before the fox hunt, when she had faced a dangerous situation of a different kind. He remembered Patricia's most uncharacteristic interest in Claire's book of engravings, an interest that had pleased him so at the time, and that had prompted him to search out Claire.

The coach drew up, its gleam softened by the fog, as George stepped out, drawing his cloak more tightly around him against the chill. Lady Patricia was at home, but she kept her caller waiting for a quarter of an hour to punish him for his neglect of the past few days. Considering how long she had waited for his return, she considered the penalty very mild. As he waited, George attempted to get his thoughts in better order.

When Lady Patricia Leland finally admitted him to her presence, she was smiling. The Wedgwood-blue morning dress she wore matched her eyes, which sparkled with interest. As usual, she was perfectly poised. George felt an aching sense of loss.

"My lord! You have finally seen fit to honor me with a visit, I see. You never told me what business sent you to the country!"

"Not worthy of your notice, my lady," George mumbled.

"How does your ward go on?" Patricia's curiosity had gotten the better of her. In other circumstances, he would not suppose it more than routinely polite.

"I did not see her."

"Why not? I hope you did not find her seriously ill?" Patricia's voice sounded light and disinterested. "But I must offer you some refreshment," she went on, motioning to a footman who provided them with glasses of a delicate pale wine.

"No," said George gruffly, "I had her sent away."

"Oh? May I ask where? I intended to send her a fan for her birthday."

"To a school she will find hard, I fear." George took a sip of the wine. Cool gambler's eyes regarded Lady Patricia over the cut crystal edge of his glass.

Patricia smiled. It seemed to George that her whole being seemed to lift, as if in triumph. "Is it one of those odious places where they stress deportment and force one to wear one's back in a brace?" She gave a short, brittle laugh and thought better of it. "I hope not, for her sake, but I cannot say Miss Amberly did not bring it on herself."

"I suppose she did," admitted George. "She was a

143

great deal too daring, but after all, my brother neglected her atrociously and she had little time to learn better."

"I thought it was clear that Miss Amberly had no desire to emulate her betters." Patricia tilted her head, catching the glow of the hearth fire on her guinea-gold curls. "I rather thought she had decided in advance that she would not be able to please anyone and was resolved that no one should know she wished to."

George stared into the fire, watching the log snap and crackle, but feeling no warmth at all. He was struck by the understanding in Lady Patricia's remark and felt a fleeting sorrow that such understanding could not be accompanied by compassion. He found himself wishing that he still had his cloak on. His voice was a little hoarse when he spoke. "I have been very worried about her. I suppose I should ask your advice. You are a woman. . . ."

Patricia laughed very pleasantly. "How it pains you gentlemen to ask a lady for advice!" she remarked, walking over to stand behind George's chair. She put an arm around his shoulder and began to fondle a lock of his hair. She was a little startled by his lack of response.

"I think you did the right thing," she told him softly. "Of course your ward is really too old for school now. She should have learned obedience at an early age, as I did."

"Did you?" asked George dryly. "Obedience is a virtue greatly to be desired in a wife."

"Oh, stuff," said Patricia, pulling his hair a little. "I could never cross Papa even in the slightest thing, or there would be the devil to pay. I learned that defiance of authority is foolish. It is better to find other methods to get what you want."

George turned up his face and looked deeply into Patricia's eyes. Then he drew her into his lap and kissed her. "Beautiful lady," he said in a hoarse whisper, "how do you get what you want?"

Miss Leland stretched herself and smiled. "I arrange things," she whispered back, returning his kiss.

144

"Are you utterly ruthless?"

"I am."

"And do you find your arrangements satisfactory to-day?"

Lady Patricia sat up, and then got to her feet. "What do you mean by that, my lord?"

"Just what I said. I admire obedience, but I think I prefer honesty. . . . Are you satisfied?"

"Yes . . ." Patricia did not know how she should answer. The black thought that George might perhaps suspect her machinations had at last penetrated her consciousness, and she felt horrified at what she had just said. "I was only joking, my lord. I am not really ruthless. . . ." She was unable to meet his eyes, and in that moment George knew for certain that Bettina had indeed told the truth.

George kissed her hand when he departed.

Later he informed Lord Leland by letter that a venture of his had jeopardized his whole estate, and since it was highly likely he would lose his fortune, he thought it best not to offer for Lady Patricia. Lord Cedric told his wife that, indeed, his assessment of the lad had been quite right: Ross had begun gambling again, but it was admirable in Ross to admit his foolishness and withdraw from a match that had been beyond him in the first place. Lord Leland congratulated himself on the way he had handled the business.

Lady Patricia, however, was more than a little upset, so much so, in fact, that Lord Cedric was led to suppose that perhaps her affections had been engaged after all.

Chapter 24

The fog was so thick it muffled the bells calling the faithful to worship at evensong. Claire's angelic appearance, in her white lace-trimmed surplice went unappreciated as the pews were largely empty. Her cool gray eyes were troubled as she listened to the responses from the choir stalls. There was no coughing to mar them this evening, since Tony had been told to stay home until he was better. Without his salary, they would have to exist on even less. There would be no hot bath for her, that was certain, let alone the wherewithal to hire a doctor, or even dose the lad with hot lemonade punch, as Bennett had done to Beaugency. Claire remembered sitting before the kitchen fire with her ailing governess, holding her mug between her knees and listening to Beaugency's stories. Now Beaugency was dead.

Claire swung the censer. She put the candles out slowly and reverently, one by one, retired to the vestry, and let herself out into the thickest fog she had ever seen. Six paces away from the church door she looked back, and it was no longer there.

At the vegetable stalls that night the customers had to bend low over the merchandise to ascertain its quality, or lack of it. Because Will's reputation was good, his stock sold early to those too lazy to do this. He disappeared into the fog, and Claire could not follow him for fear of becoming lost. She gathered up some crates, broken in a collision of wagons that had taken place that evening, and made her way along the street very slowly. Places that had been recognizable to her even in the blackest night seemed strange in their heavily shrouded state. She hesitated at every step, now chilled by uncertainty as to her location, now reassured by a landmark such as the feeble lights within the "Pharaoh," which revealed a glimpse of its worn marble steps. There was no one about, and sounds seemed muffled, as if everything were further away than usual. Clutching the wood harshly, she stumbled into a prone form, dropped the wood, and fell on her knees against the hulk.

"Jesus' name!" she swore—or prayed, she wasn't quite sure which. Was it a corpse or a living man whose bulk had barred her course? Was it his reeking breath she heard or her own pounding in her chest? The huge, heavy man proved alive, but desperately drunk. She could tell by the feel of his coat that he was a gentleman. It was unusual to find one alone in this neighborhood even by day, but perhaps his weight had discouraged his comrades from giving him the assistance he deserved. Claire felt with uneasy fingers in the man's pockets, but soon found that he'd already been robbed.

Claire then took out her knife and cut off all the silver buttons that were not out of reach under his body, and put them into her pocket. Then she took his wig, which would bring a few pennies, and got hold of her wood again. She nudged the leviathan at her feet with the muddy toe of her shoe. It would not do to let the poor fool freeze. "Sir!" shouted Claire. "Get up! The house is on fire!" As the man began to waken, she took herself off to a safe distance. He was hidden by the fog before she could see if he had made it to his feet or not.

When Claire entered Will's room she heard laughter and odd sounds from within. There was no candle to light the scene—only a weak glow from the embers of the fire Will had made. Claire dropped the wood and the wig in surprise at the sight of Lucy's exposed legs.

"Ooh, Will, what's that?" Startled at the crash of wood, Lucy tried to pull her skirts down.

"Carl?" called Will.

"Carl. I'm leaving," answered Claire in a higher, more uncertain voice than usual.

"Don't. I'll get 'er t' do it with you, too, if you want," offered Will.

Claire turned and slammed out. It was disturbing to think of Will as a man. Perhaps . . . She ran down to the stable, where she begged Joseph to let her stay until morning. He warned her not to make a habit out of it, but did not force her to leave. Just then a gentleman walked in, swinging his three-tiered cape in a veritable dance of dudgeon.

"Get the bays out at once, you bastard," he said to Joseph, and they both hurried to obey, assisted by the man's servant.

"Do you know who just walked into the 'Pharaoh'?" asked the gentleman aggressively.

"No, sir," replied Joseph politely.

"Sir Obadiah Denslow, stripped of his cloak, his wig, and his buttons like a derelict vehicle!"

Claire laughed nervously at this colorful description, and the man struck out at her with his cane. She avoided the blow with easy agility.

"Knaves, you are all knaves!" said the gentleman, and climbed into his coach with a flourish.

When he had been let out through the wide gate, Joseph looked at her reproachfully. "Next time keep your bloody trap shut," he said sharply, but after a minute he was chortling to himself over what Denslow must have looked like without his wig. Claire no longer felt that it was funny. How utterly demeaning it must have been to awaken in such a shocking condition!

When Claire had found a horse blanket and wrapped herself in it for greater warmth, she closed her eyes. From behind them came the unbidden wraith of George Howard, with his intense gaze, dark brows, and sensual lips, staring her down in disapproval as he had done so often in reality. She had hoped to forget him, but it was impossible. Claire wept quietly. She had disgraced herself thoroughly in her own eyes now by becoming immersed in worse deceit than that which she had run away to avoid. Although she could not quite believe in God, she did believe in George Howard and his kind of honor. She had never known him to tell a lie, yet by holding back his feelings he had been false to his views many times. The two of them had had the same guardian, and it had been impossible to be open with Lord Edward. Still, Claire decided that George could not have taken Sir Obadiah Denslow's buttons. Claire resolved not to show the buttons to Will. It would serve him right for his activities! Perhaps she would have the courage to return them to the gentleman later.

In the dim light of the lantern, Claire counted the buttons and wrapped them in her handkerchief so they would not clink. They were sterling silver and should bring enough to pay for a suit decent enough to wear as a clerk, if she could only find a position. Already she had earned a few pennies writing Christmas letters home to the relatives of Father Giovanni's illiterate friends. To be a clerk she would have to have a cravat as well and learn how to tie it. The thought of cravats made her think of Colin Quartermayne, who had taken an hour to tie his in a Whyndam Fall, and she smiled at the memory. Of course Claire realized that to be a clerk she would have to find night housing and resign herself to the deadening boredom of the trade. To become a clerk was a sensible but unattractive prospect, and one at which her present friends would be sure to sneer. Still, it would be nice to have a choice.

When it was five o'clock, Claire washed her face and hands in cold water, combed her hair carefully, and went out to get a couple of jam rolls at the Pig and Chicken. Lucy was still nowhere to be seen and her pa was fuming. After breakfast Claire picked her way through the fog to the church for early mass, and when she had done serving, went home to find Will already in bed, but unable to sleep because Tony was so restless.

"Rot 'im," grumbled Will. "'e's like to stick 'is spoon in the wall—the little sod."

Tony turned over again. In his fever, he was oblivious to everything.

"Do you know a doctor?" asked Claire.

"Aye, but what bloody good's that?"

149

"I think I can pay a doctor if you can find one."

"'ow?"

Mrs. Burke, who for once was sober, interjected, "May God love an' keep you if y' do! My poor babe!"

Claire took her handkerchief out of her pocket and emptied the buttons onto the table. She wet the handkerchief and began wiping Tony's forehead with it. Mrs. Burke and Will went over immediately to look at the silver.

"'oldin' out on us, were you?" he growled.

Claire answered with as much calm as she could muster. "I got them last night. It did not seem exactly the moment to mention them."

"Damn' silly wig," he said, by way of capitulation.

"And what did you get, except perhaps a clap?" she retorted. Will slapped her in the ear, scooped up the buttons, and went out. He is ashamed, Claire thought, because he could not afford to help Tony himself.

The doctor came, and Tony was better in a week. Claire was teaching him to read and would write little lessons for him to copy on the backs of handbills.

Tony became well enough to resume his place in the great oratorio. Christmas came and went with no Yule log, but they did have a chicken between them and a nice pudding.

Once, at midnight, Claire thought she saw George entering White's. He was walking with a studied elegance that she was sure she recognized, even though the brim of his hat prevented her from seeing his face. The lace at his wrist reminded her of the little ball, and the way they had danced without speaking or wishing to speak. It gave her a grand feeling to see him—to know they inhabited the same city. Never again would he look at her with one eyebrow cocked up and his mouth askew in an unwilling smile. The strength of Claire's feeling for George rose within her until she could not bear it and began to run.

Several times during the next week, Claire returned to the vicinity of White's and hung about for some time, but George did not reappear. She scolded herself unmercifully for wasting her time in such a foolish way, which did her absolutely no good. It did not change anything, that she had seen him, and it would not change anything if she saw him again.

Mr. Michael Howard presented himself to Dr. Westgate that Wednesday, saying he wished to inquire after Miss Amberly's health. "What manner of illness has she?" he asked the doctor.

"I am surprised they did not tell you at Oakhaven," replied Westgate. It was crucial that he not contradict anything Ross's cousin had already heard.

"Damned rude they were. Told me nothing. If I were Ross, I would send the lot packing, blister me if I would not! But do tell me what ails the chit?"

"Miss Amberly has rheumatic fever," said Westgate.

"Rheu——what sort of ailment is that?"

"It is a fever that seriously weakens the heart," answered the doctor gravely. "That is why she must have no visitors. The slightest excitement might kill her."

So in the end, Mr. Michael Howard was forced to wait. He began to have serious doubts as to whether his informant could have been playing games with him.

Westgate rode up to London to see Lord Ross and tell him what was afoot. "Rheumatic fever, I told him," said the doctor. "Do not forget that. It is a fever that weakens the heart. I said that in case you want to say she died. I could not do the death certificate—put my name to a falsehood. I would not have lied for you at all, if I had not known you were a victim of lies from the first. Lelands make bad enemies, my lord."

Lord Ross thanked the doctor, and when Westgate had gone, tears filled George's eyes for his own bad heart, and for Claire, wherever she was, alive or dead.

Chapter 25

For greater ease of movement George had put on his tradesman's clothes to search the poorer neighborhoods. A thorough search of the hospitals, the shipping offices, the registries, and the morgue had turned up nothing. Men had been hired to inquire at factories that had been hiring people, and there were not many of these. Now, to Collins' disgust, George was preparing to search the district of flash houses.

"What shall we do if we find her here?" he asked his master.

"She will find out." The tone in which he said it made Collins hope in spite of his fatigue that their search in this quarter would not meet with success.

All through that dreary day, in and out of fourteen or more houses from those of poor but decent quality to those of the most heartbreaking and stomach-turning wretchedness, they continued to search. In every place they encountered propositions, in many, clues so blatantly false that George became aware that deceiving men like him was a common stock-in-trade. At last, feeling soiled and exhausted, he stopped at an inn and received a supper as bad as any he had ever eaten. However, when they came out of the place a young girl came up to them and introduced herself. She said she had heard they were looking for a certain blue dress.

"Do you have it?" asked Collins.

"No, sir, but I know where it is."

"Show us and you earn half a crown—if it is the dress."

"I'll show you right enough, sir," she answered, leading them through the dark streets until they reached a second-hand shop. The girl aroused the shopwoman and made her open the place, and when George saw that it was indeed the odd blue-gray dress that had been Claire's, he was delighted. If Collins had not been along, he would have kissed it.

Close questioning failed to reveal any clue to Claire's whereabouts. At last he was truly on the trail but it was now so old that his ward could be anywhere. He gave the girl her half crown, and she ran away happy. Then they had several brandies to celebrate.

Later, when he and Collins were making their way back out of the quarter, six strong youths accosted them with knives, demanding their purses. Collins made to resist, but George forbade him. "Give him your purse, Collins. Do not be an idiot." Meekly Collins handed over his money, and George did likewise. In any case there was little left of the ready money he had brought along for the day's expenses.

"'e bain't as flush as y' thought!" said a wide-faced lad in a deep slouch hat and fur-trimmed cape.

"Too bad we'll 'ave yer flash gels tonight!" The closest of them jeered, making an obscene gesture with the point of his knife.

Before Collins realized what was happening, George had caught the boy a terrible blow to the side of the head, fetching him up with a brutal crunch against the alley wall. The knife fell, and Collins dived for it at once. Blood spurted from the lad's nose. The other members of the gang stared in amazement. George sprang toward them with a growl. His sudden rage made even Collins stand away in awe. George was ready to take their knives away from them, but none thought it worth the fight. Already in possession of the money, they left their wounded cohort lying on the cobbles and made good a retreat.

Rushing after them, George found himself in the meat market. His hand began to ache. All around him were the bloody carcasses of animals. The stench was incredible. Collins caught him up. "Good God, my lord," he begged. "Haven't you had enough? Let's go

153

home." George let out a string of oaths foul enough to shock his servant and ordered Collins to go to the devil. Collins, thoroughly disgusted, walked back to Pomfret House, leaving George as much alone in fact as he was in spirit.

After wandering nearly a mile, George stopped for a couple of better brandies at a place where he had credit, but never thought of borrowing the price of a cab. Limping openly now, he dragged himself along until he saw a house he recognized. It was De Vere House, where a friendly light was burning. There George's much abused leg gave out under him and he fell to the pavement, where he lay struggling to gain control of himself. Reason told him it was a damned uncomfortable place to lie down, but he could not quite lift himself up.

Some minutes later, when Lady Diana arrived home from the opera, she was astonished to see what looked like a rangy tradesman blocking access to her door.

"I'll see to 'im, my lady," said her footman, reaching down to grasp the offending body under his arms. As the head was lifted, Lady Diana started with recognition.

"Claire, oh, God. Claire," moaned George, and was sick on the pavement.

"Bring him inside the house," commanded Lady de Vere. "Take him upstairs and put him to bed. And have Dawes run over to Pomfret House and tell Collins that his master is here and will stay the night."

The footman stared in open disbelief, but he knew better than to question the Lady Diana.

When George woke in one of Lady de Vere's immaculate beds, Collins was waiting outside his door with clean things. When George appeared at breakfast he presented a signal contrast to his appearance the previous night. His hair, allowed to fall further than usual across his forehead quite neatly concealed the nasty bruise he had received, but a slight pallor and scarcely perceptible look of tension showed Lady Diana that he was still not quite himself.

Diana was seated in the breakfast room, looking

relaxed and fresh in a muslin dress sprigged with the same lavender as the chrysanthemums on her table. It did not show that she had been waiting there an hour for George to appear.

George kissed her hand. "Thank you for your kindness, my lady. You spared me a most uncomfortable night."

Diana smiled warmly up into his worried eyes. "I could not have you decorating the walk at that early hour. At four o'clock perhaps, but *not* at ten."

"I cannot have been very decorative," he answered.

She wrinkled her nose. "It was not your appearance that surprised me, my lord. I simply wonder what took you so long."

"What took me so long?" George looked truly bewildered.

"You are in love."

"No!" He said it vehemently, setting down his cup only half-filled. "The marriage is off. You know that."

"Do not think you can hide behind that Leland nonsense anymore," warned Diana severely. "Whose name was on your lips last night?"

George felt so alone and unhappy that he could easily have burst into tears. He sat down and put his hands over his ears. How much had he said?

"You are serious," said Diana doggedly, "and I want to know what is wrong. Perhaps I could help you."

George knew that Diana had a real regard for him. He had certainly achieved nothing acting alone. "If you would give me your word of honor not to tell . . ." he began.

"Women," said Desmarais brightly, entering the room, "do not have any honor."

"Oh! We have as much honor as you do. Now please go away, Darcy," said his sister, with some heat.

"Sorry to ruin your *tête-à-tête*," said Desmarais lightly, "but if you must pick up drunks, I'd prefer not to have them spoil my breakfast." He turned to fill his plate from the buffet. When he faced the others again, he could see that George was blushing, but before further comment could be made George left

155

the room. He went out into the street without his cloak, and Collins followed him with it. From the window Lady Diana watched him stop to put it on. Her brother sat down calmly to eat his plate of eggs. Diana's gaze left the window and turned toward her brother's lounging form. It was a few moments before he noticed her regard and raised his indolent glance to meet it. He was caught by an unaccustomed hardness in her eyes.

"Darcy, if you are to stay at my house, you must be civil to my guests!" she admonished him.

"To Howard? Oh, fustain! When have you ever cared for the way I tease him? He *was* shot in the neck, you know, and he need not ask you to keep it quiet, for it is certain Leland will find out—that is, if anyone recognized him, which it is possible they did not, in that quizzy coat he had on."

"You callous, unfeeling lout," said his sister with conviction. "You sail in with no sensibility and less knowledge of the situation. Ross does not care two straws what Leland thinks now. He cried off two weeks ago. I should say, I found out about it two weeks ago."

A look of wonder came across Desmarais' face. "I would not have thought he was celebrating his escape," he said lightly.

"He was about to tell me when you had to barge in!" said Diana sharply.

"Now, Di," he answered patiently, "you know you are in a miff because I have prevented you from finding out what is none of your affair."

"Good morning," said Diana fiercely and went upstairs.

Outside, in the park, Collins approached his master cautiously and handed him his cloak. "I'm sorry, my lord," he muttered. "Should have stuck with you, no matter how you set me down." George took the cloak absently and put it on. Several gulls alighted on the far side of the park. "Looks like a storm, for sure," said the valet nervously.

"Aye. It will snow before afternoon, I fancy," said

George. He was trying to remain collected, but realizing it was useless to try to hide his loss of composure from Collins, turned to face his man. "If I was floored at all points last night, it was what I deserved for sending you away," he admitted. George's voice was deep and rough. Collins knew how he hated to admit to being wrong about anything.

"Come on home," he said gently, "you're burned to the socket, for all you've slept," and George Howard let Collins lead him to Pomfret House, where he fell into a restive doze in the library chair.

George dreamed that he saw Claire, in her muslin dress, running through the home wood. He started after her, but his leg started to give way, each step being more difficult than the last. . . .

Chapter 26

It was raining hard and getting colder. Claire pulled
her cap down over her ears as she hurried through
the streets. It was a theater opening night, and she
meant to present herself at the stable to see if there
was extra work to do. Joseph told her that there was
not much now, but that she should return just before
the end of the show. Claire decided to walk around to
the theater, as she often did, and watch the swells go
in from the shelter of the portico across the street.

After a few moments, a gleaming black coach drew
up, drawn by four gorgeous black horses, and a man
got out, accompanied by two violet-caped young
ladies, who ducked their heads against the rain. Following the ladies as they scurried up the steps to shelter, the man turned back for a moment with seeming
reluctance and scanned the busy street behind him.
His briefly revealed profile was that, unmistakably, of
George Howard. Claire wondered with pleasure why
it was not Lady Patricia he was escorting.

After a short visit to the vegetable market, Claire
returned to the stable. There, much to her surprise,
was the Ross coach, aligned with the others. It was
probable that George had had Hawkins leave it there
for him to drive home himself, as he often preferred
to do.

Stealthily, Claire opened the gleaming black door.
Inside, the coach smelled of leather, of George's snuff,
and faintly of some fine perfume. Claire fell into a
reverie, remembering the time she had driven with
George to the dressmaker, and how he had said to
her, "The little girl you were is now dead." It was as
if this coach were in mourning as she had been—with-

out grief, but with respect. Claire closed her eyes. It was a luxury to imagine Oakhaven. Inexplicably, she fell asleep. Outside, the rain began to freeze.

George was escorting the Knight sisters to the play as a favor to Lady Diana. As an attempt on her part to distract him from his worries, it had been well meant but a signal failure. After the performance was over, Lord Ashton invited the Knight sisters and a small party of others to his house for supper. Knowing them to be in good hands and not really being in the mood to enjoy himself in that staid company, George bade them good night. In spite of the freezing rain, he walked to the African, and watched the play for some time. Since he did not have to concentrate, he drank far more brandy than he should have. At length he became bored and decided to leave.

As George went out into the frosty night, he drew his cape closer around him. The icy air sobered him a trifle and he remembered to walk properly toward the stables, although there was no one about to see whether he limped or not. He was foxed, yes—but not so addled that he could not drive his rig. It was only a short walk to the stables, but the wind cut his face like a steel blade. The cobblestones had become covered with sheet ice and had to be negotiated with care. In front of the stables, the old cherry tree was bent under a shiny sheath that covered every twig. It caught the lamplight like a crystal chandelier. George struck his hat against it, and tiny pieces of ice fell tinkling at his feet. He stared at them, thinking of the broken shards on the flags of the ruined church, where Claire's glass king lay scattered.

If a fierce gust of wind, cold enough to make his ears and teeth ache had not propelled him on, George might have remained there for some time lost in thought.

The stable seemed warm and dark by contrast. Joseph was dozing, but he got up immediately to put the horses to.

Claire woke with the lurch of the coach as it began

159

to move. Suddenly realizing where she was, she leaped down at once. George saw the blurred form of an urchin in dirty tweeds jolt to earth and run groggily for the doors. Joseph was angry. He had never given Carl permission to sleep in the coaches! "Filthy encroachin' beggar!" he shouted, giving chase.

Claire did not expect sheet ice on the ground. Her feet flew out from under her, and she fell hard. Her cap was knocked off, and catching the wind, fetched up against the board wall at the end of the stable yard. Claire swore with feeling. Joseph drew back his foot to kick the prostrate figure, but was restrained by the unexpected touch of a soft glove on his arm.

"I know this lad," said Lord Ross.

The gutter obscenities died on Claire's lips. They could not defend her from recognition now. Staring down at her were two restless eyes that missed nothing. Joseph reached down and hauled her roughly to her feet. Claire faced George with all the bravado of a cornered bandit chief.

"So you wanted to ride in my coach?" said George slowly. "Well, you shall. Put him up on the box, Joseph, where I can keep an eye on him, and I will take him home."

Claire struggled with the ostler as he hoisted her up onto the box. Joseph said, "The dirty little beggar was like to steal something, my lord. I'd 'ave 'im taken up if I was you."

"He will be taken up if he deserves it," said George airily as they drove off. Claire's tawny curls were blown away from her face by the bitter wind. She gripped the seat and clenched her teeth so he would not hear them chatter. George Howard is really drunk this time, she thought. I have never seen him drive so aimlessly before.

In fact, George did not quite know where to take his find. It was out of the question to go to his house, where the servants would surely talk of the matter, nor could he bring her to Lady de Vere's house dressed like that! Still, atrocious and inexplicable as Claire's conduct had been, George could not help

160

being drawn to her as strongly as ever before—drawn by her fragility and her crazy courage.

"So I am to be taken up," she said at length.

"I meant by me," said her captor grimly. "You have some explaining to do, little whore. I ought to . . ."

Claire stood up as if she meant to leap from the box. She wanted to jump rather than face his contempt. George could see confusion on her face and regretted his words, but could not slow his horses without their change of pace throwing the girl off balance. Instead, he reached up with one hand and pulled her straight down on the seat next to him.

"Keep still," he said fiercely. "If you fall, you may knock your teeth out."

At that moment George knew he could wait no longer. He decided to take Claire to the Boar and Ring, where he was a known patron, and the discretion of the staff was close to perfect. Once resolved, he began to move the rig with purpose through the empty streets.

Outside the hotel he stopped and helped his pale shivering passenger down from the box. George removed his cape and wrapped it around her. Only then did he realize how cold she must have felt during the journey. He placed his beaver hat on her head. "Keep the cape tightly around you, or it will get around that I have developed a taste for boys." George's voice was light, but his grip on Claire's wrist was like iron as he steered her through the entry, and with the clerk in tow, up the stairs to a room. George told the clerk to send up a bath, and then supper, and only when the room door was closed did he release her arm.

The room in which they found themselves was a comfortable one, with a fire already burning in the grate. George took his beaver hat from her and hung it up while servants brought a tub and screen into the chamber.

As the fire began to bring color to her cheeks and reason to her mind, Claire Amberly knew she was bad. She knew what kind of hotel this was, and what George must think of her to bring her here. After all,

161

he had said it. As she stared at the gorgeous tongues of flame dancing around the logs on the hearth, she knew she did not care if what was going to happen brought her to hell fire or not. George would never believe she was still a virgin unless she let him have his way with her, and when he had done, she would be what he had called her—a whore.

Claire's reverie was broken by the entrance of servants with her bath. It was no wonder George did not want to touch her until she was clean. After hanging her tweeds over the screen and unwrapping the rag with which her breasts were bound, she began seriously to wash off the stubborn grime, and did not notice when her things disappeared. George had taken them out silently and disposed of them in the nearest dustbin. On the way back he engaged a boy to go 'round to his house and have Collins fetch Claire's trunk and his own morning clothes to the Boar and Ring before dawn.

When George returned to the room, he found Claire wearing a bedsheet draped in the Roman manner. She looked quite elegant in this simple garb, which did not attempt to embellish what could not be improved.

A servant bearing a tray of food knocked at the door and was admitted. Suddenly determined that the servant should not think anything out of the way, George gazed at his ward and drawled, "Yes. That should be the very thing for Lady de Vere's masquerade . . . like those headless women, the Elgin marbles!"

"And what shall you be, my lord?" returned Claire.

"Emperor Nero, of course." He grinned as the servant went out.

"Then shall I be headless, too?" she asked, looking gravely up at him. From a dirty, shivering child she had transformed herself into a beautiful woman. There was no more defiance in her eyes, only a trace of contempt, whether for herself or for him, George could not guess.

They sat down to eat. George was not hungry but attempted to disguise the fact. Claire ate silently because she was hungry and ashamed. George did not

162

speak either, because he found he could not bring himself to ask for the explanation he had so much desired. He watched her intently, curiously, and a little more soberly until Claire could not bear his eyes anymore. Distracted, she had let the sheet slip a little from around her breast.

"What do you want from me, George?" she asked.

"I will show you," he answered, and taking her into his arms, kissed her with great force and hunger. Claire could feel her whole body tremble in the power of his kiss. Held close by his strong arms she struggled in fear. These feelings were too strange, too intense. Then suddenly he let her go.

Her lips parted as she listened to the sounds of his elegant clothes being tossed carelessly aside. She thought, with something close to panic, that she did not know what she should do and regretted that she had never stayed to watch Will with Lucy. A whore should not be afraid to look. Claire forced herself to open her eyes. George must not think her afraid of him.

George ignored these signs of modesty in his little actress, and he proceeded to make passionate love to her. When he entered her, he was surprised to feel resistance and hear a stifled cry of pain. By then it was too late to stop. After he had finished and the tangled covers had been pulled up around them, he felt a great surge of tenderness for this girl who had chosen not to defend her honor. He reached over to caress her hand, kiss her fingertips and her hair. Then sleep overtook them, the fire burned down, and a bitter chill began to penetrate the room. George and Claire turned in their sleep toward each other for warmth. George's touch woke Claire just long enough for her to wonder at the tenderness she felt from him.

Chapter 27

The gray dawn had not yet shown itself above London, but Claire Amberly lay in George Howard's arms. For a long time, wide awake as she was, she could not bear to move and end this closeness that was so wonderful to her. Working at the vegetable market it had become natural for her to be awake all night, and as she lay there savoring George's presence she told herself that it would be better not to stay with him. What could he do with a despicable creature like her, after all? Unfit by birth to be a man, and unfit by education to be a true woman, she could be of no real use to him. George had been drunk. Surely in the morning he would regret what he had done, and be relieved that she had gone.

Once resolved, Claire got up quickly, and gathered George's scattered evening clothes to see if there was something she could wear. She observed that Collins had left George's morning clothes on a chair, but did not notice her trunk, because Collins had placed it behind the screen. Standing before the little glass, she washed herself, combed her hair with George's silver comb, and belted in his satin trousers with his cravat. It is lucky he forgot to chuck my shoes, she thought. I could scarcely wear his. Then Claire pocketed half the coins from his purse and stood poised to go. Carts were going by in the street, but it was not yet sunrise.

George Howard lay in the mahogany bedstead, covered by the white quilt. All the impatience, the teasing grins, and smoldering frowns that had played over his face were wiped away by sleep. Morpheus gave George a gentle, even vulnerable look. The sa-

ber-cut on his cheek no longer seemed a badge of arrogance, but a wound suffered by a boy.

Claire had the irresistible desire to touch it very
lightly in farewell. As she passed her finger over his
cheek he stirred, and she found her wrist imprisoned
in a gentle, powerful grip, that forced her slowly to
her knees, where her captor could fix her better in his
sleepy gaze.

"Let me go," she demanded. His grip did not
budge.

"You ought to be flogged."

"For stealing your clothes?" He had no right to be
angry about that. After all, he had taken hers.

"No. For bad taste. You look ridiculous."

"Beggars can't be choosers," she said, touching the
heavy satin of the breeches with one hand while trying determinedly to haul the other out of his fist.
"Good-bye, George."

"Do not go," he grinned, struggling with her, and as
he did so the coins in her pocket jingled loudly.

"So!" he said, jerking her into his lap. "You mean to
leave me without a feather to fly with! Well, you
may not go on behaving like a whore, now that you
have shown you are not one!" He began, unforgiva-
bly, to rifle her pockets.

"But, George, I did not take it all. Oh!" she protested, and when he had successfully extracted the
money, she ceased fighting him.

"You have desecrated my third best cravat." George
was undoing the knot at Claire's waist with his long
hard fingers. "Your trunk is behind that screen. When
you leave here, it will be dressed as a lady."

"That will not make me one," she retorted, pulling
away from him.

"You shall be Lady Ross, Claire, if you wish it."

"I did not do it for that," she said dryly.

"I doubt that you did it because you were contemplating life as a tart. Haven't you noticed that I love
you?"

Her eyes were black as she looked up at him.
"Nothing will happen," she said. "You will forget me

like the others." George raised his hand and slapped her suddenly and hard.

"You are not like the others," he added, feeling rather shocked that she had taken his cruel blow without wincing or crying out. As Claire retreated behind the screen, he reached for his morning clothes. Claire's cheek was burning.

"At least I have the distinction of being the person you are beastliest to," she grumbled and threw open the trunk.

George peeked over the screen where Claire's trunk now lay open. She was wide-eyed at the discovery of the blue dress she had pawned. This was proof of his devotion more forcible than any words could be. "I can understand your refusing my offer, since I really have been beastly to you," he said softly, "but I cannot allow you to leave until you have told me where I can find you again. I cannot bear never to see you, Claire. You must have some reason for behaving as you did last night!"

Claire looked up. George was beginning to look dangerous again. "If you are promised to Lady Patricia, how can you offer for me?" she said doubtfully.

"I forgot. Of course, you could not have heard. I cried off a month ago. It was never in the *Gazette*, after all."

"You cried off? What for?"

"She used lies and deceit to get you into trouble. I could see that she would stop at nothing to wind me completely about her thumb, and I could not endure that. I was very much mistaken in her character."

"But if you knew it was all lies, how could you not tell me? That was cruel. You never wrote one word. . . ." Claire's voice caught.

"I did not know it myself until after you left Oakhaven. Lady Patricia must have destroyed your letters as they arrived at Leland House, so I never knew you had written. I have been looking for you ever since—even in the flash houses. It was driving me mad."

Claire looked at him with suspicion and disbelief.

166

"I used to see you sometimes. You went to the theater and to your club. I watched you go in."

George gave her his most piercing look. "Why?"

"I wanted to see you. I could not do that at Oakhaven." Her eyes were gentle at last, and in them he read an admission that she did care for him.

George pushed the screen aside and stood beside the kneeling girl. "I will take you to stay with Lady de Vere," he offered. "I wanted you to marry me, but it would be better for you to marry someone who is not so old—someone with two good legs."

Claire reached up and kissed his bad knee. "I love your legs," she whispered.

George took her tawny head in his fingers and turned her face up to his. "But you looked so horrified when I was running in the quarry. . . ."

"Stuff." She laughed. "You forget, you were glaring at me and holding that whip. You had probably forgotten you had it in your hand."

George took his hands away. "I have been a brute, Claire."

"I guess I do have bad taste, George, to love a brute," and she brushed his cheek with her lips.

"Your punishment will be that you will have to take me." His voice lowered to a hoarse whisper. "Please, Claire, take me."

Claire smiled, "Yes, George, yes." Then George drew his fiancée up close to his body and held her between his knees to kiss her.

Later, after they made love, Claire dressed herself in her best chemise and petticoat, and selected her warmest pelisse, as she no longer had a jacket or a cloak to put on. She emerged at last from behind the screen shod in dainty slippers and went to the mirror to comb her hair. It looked substantially worse with a dress, she decided. The newly washed ends were flying every which way. She felt restless under George's appraising eyes.

"You have probably made me lose my place," she told him.

A slow smile crossed his lips. "What place?" he inquired.

"Promise me you will not laugh."

"Why should I laugh?"

Claire looked away from him. Over his shoulder in the glass she could see his grave, sweet smile, as she dragged the comb through her stubborn curls again.

"I was an altar boy," she said. Behind her face she could see his grin break as he laughed at her.

Instantly she whirled around to slap him and found her wrist seized and held only an inch from his face. "You can not have lived on what you made doing that," he observed, his lips brushing her forehead.

"Let me go!" she struggled, only to have her other hand trapped and her body drawn close to his.

"Tell me what else you did."

"I wrote letters for a ha'penny in English or Italian. I sold vegetables at the market. I held and curried horses at the stable where you found me—and I stole. . . ."

"Claire, I must take you to Natalie's. Your hair is such a quiz. . . ." he interrupted.

Angrily, Claire pulled herself free of his slackened grip and retorted, "Do you care more for my coiffure or for my morals?"

"Well, the coiffure is more susceptible to amendment, but I promise I will thrash you if I catch you stealing. Are you satisfied? I should thrash you as it is. Were you not afraid you would end in Bridewell?"

"Yes, but I was hungrier than I was afraid."

"I do not want you ever to be that hungry again. Now put on your bonnet, and we shall go to breakfast." George was looking at her sternly but his eyes were smiling.

Claire picked up her bonnet and put it on. She felt very much ashamed of having been a thief. As if he were reading her mind, George said, "I had to steal to eat, too, sometimes, in the army." He put his arm around her and they left the room. She felt it was a miracle that she should be so completely forgiven. It had to be a dream from which she should soon be rudely awakened. It crossed her mind that perhaps Desmarais had recognized her. It was a quelling thought, but it was soon lost in the pleasure of discovering a side of London she had only dreamed existed. Her delight in the delicious pastries, the coffee, the fashionable coiffure, and the beautiful beaver-trimmed cloak George bought her was distracting. So was the sheer excitement of his company, the thrill of being permitted to touch him, to take his arm, and run the gauntlet of a hundred curious eyes.

When they drove through the park, it was much warmer. Ice dripped from the trees as the sun struck sparks from every twig.

"Kiss me," he ordered her. "I will not have the opportunity to do anything improper once I have left you with Lady de Vere."

Claire kissed him easily enough, but George could tell something was bothering her. He frowned, and took her by the shoulders. "What is it?" he inquired.

"Could you leave me somewhere else?" she whispered.

"What are you afraid of? I certainly do not mean to inform your hostess of your exploits. Once I almost told her you had bolted, but Darcy interrupted me. I am glad now that he did. I told everyone who asked me that you were ill at Oakhaven with rheumatic fever. You have a weak heart, so do not be too impetuous," he told her, fondling her newly trimmed curls.

"It is Viscount Desmarais," she admitted, her face white. "He. . ."

"Darcy? He will mind his manners." Claire looked doubtful. Desmarais was perfectly irrepressible, and she knew it. "If he does not, I shall call *him* out," answered George hotly, holding her close. "I love you, and he can not hurt you."

Claire's terror rose in her again but she told herself that perhaps Desmarais would not be at home. Perhaps her new hairstyle would put her past his recognition. In any case, she must summon the courage to face them, or she could never have George. He had said that he loved her, and she did not wish to refuse him anything.

The coach pulled up to Lady de Vere's front door.

"Are you up to the rig, little villain?" he whispered, and she was able to manage a shaky smile.

When Lady Diana's butler ushered Lord Ross and his ward into the room, Lady Diana rose from the tea table, came forward, and took the girl's hand in welcome. "Miss Amberly, I am delighted that you could come to visit us at last," she said. "How do you like London?"

"I am happy to be here, thank you. London is a bit dirty, but I have not really seen the better parts yet."

George gave her a hard look, and Claire broke off. "It is kind of you to have me," she stammered.

Then Lady Diana introduced Claire to Lady Devereux and Lady Pendleton. "Your hair is beautiful, my dear," said Lady Pendleton, eyeing George coldly. "I have been thinking of having my own cut in just such a style. Can you tell me where you had it . . . ?" At that moment Desmarais broke into the room.

"Di!" he shouted, "I have just seen the most famous fight!" His fists were up, and he danced over to George in a pugilistic stance, jabbing at the air. Claire in sudden terror had ducked behind George's back. She was sure that if she had had the bad fortune to be holding a cup she would surely have dropped it.

"Howard, you dog!" said Desmarais with mock belligerence. "It's Miss Amberly! Where have you been hiding her?" He threw a shadow punch at his friend. George raised one eyebrow, and aimed a series of feints at his opponent, so fast and accurate that it was clear what the outcome of a real mill would have been. Desmarais backed off, and the ladies laughed.

Desmarais saw Claire peeking curiously from behind George. He smiled at her. "I have been ill," she explained.

"A fever that affects the heart you said it was, my lord?" asked Diana. George nodded.

"She does look pale," commented Lady Devereux.

"I think I was really too brown to be elegant before," stated Miss Amberly with pretended nonchalance.

"We mean to be married very soon," said George

unexpectedly, "so if you are going to achieve elegance you had best do it by then."

"You and Claire?" shouted Desmarais. "Why, that is perfect!" and slipping past George's guard he put his hand on Claire's waist and swung her off her feet, in a dizzy arc.

"Have a care, sir!" snapped Lady Pendleton. "The lady has been ill!"

Desmarais stopped spinning her about. "You are drunk, my lord," grinned Claire.

"And rude as usual. But my congratulations." He turned to George. "You have always wanted the ones out of your reach and left off wanting each one as soon as you knew you could have her. Now I know why you waited. Really worth waiting for, I should say."

Lord Ross took Miss Amberly by the hand to accept the congratulations of the others. He could feel her fingers trembling within his, and felt as if he were already one with her, sharing her wild fear and fierce joy. George will never really have her, thought Desmarais dreamily. He will go on wanting her all his life.

About the Author

MADELINE GIBSON began writing regency romances after she picked up one her daughter was reading, read it and said, "I could write one better than that"—and did. An avid artist and traveler, she now spends much of her non-writing time working with stained glass. Ms. Gibson, who has a BA from Brown and a Masters from Rutgers, lives in New Jersey with her three children.